Also by Amanda Hamm

ROMANCE ARTS
*The Art of Introductions* (# 1)
*The Art of Patience* (# 2)
*The Art of Communication* (#3)
*The Art of Friendship* (#4)
*The Art of Proposing* (ebook short stories)

LOVE IN ANDAUK
*Everything Old* (#1)
*Into the Fire* (#2)
*By Its Cover* (#3)
*What Goes Around* (#4)

*They See a Family*
*The Study Group* (ebook novella)

COFFEE AND DONUTS
*Said and Unsaid* (#1)
*Sofie Waits* (#2)
*A Perfectly Good Man* (#3)
*Not Complicated* (#4)

STORIES FROM HARTFORD
*Andrew's Key* (#1)
*Jealousy & Yams* (#2)
*Collecting Zebras* (#3)
*The Christmas Project* (#4)
*Hearts on the Window* (ebook novella)

*Beyond Wisherton* (#1)
*Back to Wisherton* (#2)
*Brelin and Wisherton* (#3)
*Baby of Wisherton* (#4)
*Birthdays and Wisherton* (#5)

# Evelyn's Granddaughter

## More Love in Andauk #1

Amanda Hamm

*I* stared at my signature after I wrote it. A signature used to feel super significant, yet mine was becoming commonplace. I'd lost count of the number of documents I'd signed in the last two weeks. I read everything and hoped I understood enough. The only thing I knew with certainty though, was that God was still with me in this sea of change. He was the reason my head was still above the water.

"Now this one." My lawyer tapped her finger where I needed to sign next.

I glanced at my mom, who smiled encouragingly.

A trowel continued to scrape loudly against the wall as Mr. Franks finished his work. Plaster marked the outline, but he had done very well. Once it was painted, no one would be able to tell a door used to be there.

"Cassidy?" My mom continued to smile pleasantly and shared a commiserating look with my lawyer as though I was daydreaming and not struggling to process everything that was happening.

"I know," I said. My hand stayed still. Mrs. Sweet, my lawyer, had been extremely patient as she'd explained terms and answered my many questions. I didn't want to make her wait longer than necessary. I only needed a few more seconds for my heart to catch up to this commitment. Just because the entrance was on the outside now didn't mean I *had* to rent the apartment to someone else. He was going to pay me more than I was paying to live somewhere else, somewhere else that was still nearby. It felt overly complicated, but it didn't feel wrong. I signed the last form.

"And that's it." Mrs. Sweet closed her laptop and began to collect all the paperwork. "You officially have two tenants now." She glanced over her shoulder at Sarah Franks.

Sarah was sitting by her flowers. She had no customers and was trying to pretend she couldn't hear everything that was going on a few feet away. I was nervous about how the two of us would share the space after our rocky start.

"Simon Donnolly is a good kid though," Mrs. Sweet continued. "You have nothing to worry about."

I wasn't worried about Simon. I'd only met him for about five minutes, but he seemed normal. I had no reason to suspect he might destroy an apartment. Plus, I knew his mom was very active at the church. That had to be a point towards him having decent character, even beyond Mrs. Sweet's endorsement. And with the outside entrance, I didn't expect to have much contact with him anyway. My only worry was that he'd think I was a terrible landlord.

Mrs. Sweet had gathered everything into her bag, but she didn't rush to the door. "I'm sorry again for your loss." She moved her eyes to include my mom. "Your mom and grandma was a wonderful lady who will be missed. We're all glad she left her shop in such capable hands."

"Thank you," I said. She was the only one who hadn't batted an eye at Granny's Shelf being run by an inexperienced twenty-three-year-old. My gratitude was sincere even though I wasn't sure I believed what she said.

"Don't forget you can call me if you think of any more questions," Mrs. Sweet said before she stepped aside to exchange a few pleasantries with Mr. Franks on her way out.

My mom turned to me. "Are you sure about all this?"

I wasn't sure about anything. Except God. I just raised my eyebrows at her.

"The shop, the new apartment, the guardianship, quitting your job… you sure you've made the right decision about all this?"

"Um…" I didn't know how to answer, mostly because I didn't feel I'd made any decisions to be sure about. Granny had made the decisions in her will. Mom had coached me on how to accept it all. Her question didn't seem to be about past decisions but about whether or not I was ready to take over future decisions. I was ready. It didn't entirely make sense to me to feel ready, but God didn't always make sense. He was the source of my confidence. "Yeah, Mom. I think I'll be fine."

Mom smiled while her eyes pooled with tears. "Granny knew you'd handle it. And Ava will get over it soon. She's happy as a nurse, and… I think grief is clouding her emotions."

I nodded and hoped she was right about my sister. We weren't particularly close, but I still wanted to have some sort of relationship with her.

"David and I will be there at 1 o'clock sharp with the truck."

3

"I know. Most of my stuff is already in boxes so I shouldn't have any trouble being ready for you."

"Cool. I need to run now." She pulled me in for a quick hug and reached the door just behind Mrs. Sweet.

Mr. Franks had packed up his tools. "You sure you don't want me to paint this for you? I could do it lickety-split."

"No, thanks," I said. "I got that." I had no idea how to move a door so his help was a necessary expense. But I could handle a paintbrush. Mom had been right to negotiate a lower price that left me with the finishing touch.

"All right. Let me give you the keys." He held out a ring with three keys on it. "These two that are the same, that's for the door outside. The odd one is for your new place. I figure it's easier to give that to you now so you don't wait on me tomorrow."

I studied the perfect wall behind him. "There's no need for you to come back tomorrow."

"Not this place," he said on a chuckle. "The place you're renting from me."

I was renting my new apartment from Mr. Franks? I guessed my mom had somehow left out that important detail. My eyes flashed to Sarah, who smiled hesitantly at us. She clearly knew I was renting from her dad before I did. I was already just a tiny bit afraid of her, and this new blow didn't help. "Thank you," I said. I grasped my new keys in a tight fist.

"Do you want to try those out before I leave?"

I knew he was offering to let me inspect his work. A chip in my confidence was trying to suggest he might not believe I was capable of using the key without instructions. "I'm sure you tested them," I said.

4

He nodded. "Until tomorrow then, Miss Bodner."

I said, "Goodbye," and watched Mr. Franks leave. He and Sarah waved at each other when he was pushing open the door. I continued staring at the door as it closed. It was a glass door with Granny's Shelf in white scripty letters. They were backwards from my current perspective. They were familiar but maybe not familiar enough. I could have visited more often.

I squashed that regret before it could fully form. Granny knew I loved her. I had made time for her, and questioning whether or not it was enough time would do no good now. It would do even less good than watching the unmoving white letters. When I thought about what I should be doing, I realized that Sarah had been watching me do nothing.

She quickly turned to the door, probably not to stare at the letters but to hope a customer would appear to rescue us from the tense silence.

I didn't know if there was anything I could say to convince her I wouldn't be a terrible landlord. Was that even the right word? I knew I'd read it in books. I liked historical fiction where landlords were usually greedy men who owned large tenements. Did it apply in current times to a person who owned one building? When had I last heard it in real life? I guessed it didn't matter if I didn't intend to call myself that. I guessed I'd called myself landlord in my head a few times. No one else knew that. I didn't need a title for my tenants to think I was terrible at the job. One of them was looking at me again. She appeared to be on the verge of saying something.

Should I say something first? Did I need to apologize again for the days she couldn't sell any flowers? Or the ones that died? Nothing would ease my conscience and bringing it up might just

5

pour salt in her wounds. What I really needed to do was stop standing stock still in the middle of the shop like I didn't have a clue.

"I'll, um, I guess I'll get some paint," I said.

"She didn't want to take any money at all," Sarah blurted.

"Granny?"

"Yeah, she… your grandma offered to let me set up here for free. I had to talk her into taking anything."

"Oh." I took a moment to process that, or to try to figure out why Sarah told me. Mrs. Sweet had suggested I could charge Sarah much more than the ten dollars a month she currently paid. I guessed she wanted me to know she hadn't taken advantage of my grandmother or she didn't want me to raise the rent. "I know Granny was generous," I said. "And I don't want to make any immediate changes. I need time to… to make the place feel like mine before I… The rent is fine for now."

Sarah dropped her eyes to the floor. She knew she had a bargain, and I hadn't reassured her it would last.

I wanted to say something else. I couldn't make promises before I fully understood the situation. Granny wrote everything down. Her financial records were detailed and would be a big help to me. But I only knew that because Mrs. Sweet had told me. I hadn't been able to bring myself to open any of Granny's personal account books. It felt too much like snooping. If I was going to run her business, I'd need to get over that hurdle sooner rather than later.

"I'll get the paint," I said. I had one concrete job. I didn't know how to fix the awkward conversation, but I knew how to fix the wall.

Sarah nodded. She actually looked grateful we were done talking for the moment. We'd found common ground, though I doubted it was something to build on.

I took a circuitous path towards the back, browsing glass shelves full of fragile items. Some things were new, some had been there for years, including the ceramic frog with the bulging eyes. Granny loved the unique items and was happiest to sell those. Farther in were the knickknacks that featured Lake Erie sites or simply the words Lake Erie. Those were Granny's bread-and-butter, especially during the summer tourist season.

There was an old school locker on the back wall, no locks. Granny kept a few personal items there while she was in the shop. When I opened it to retrieve my purse, I paused at the sight of Granny's sweater still on a hook. Had she hung that there the day she died? It could have been a spare she hadn't worn in months.

I slipped the purse strap across my body and closed the locker. I closed it gently and cringed at the metal-on-metal clang anyway. The acoustics of Granny's Shelf had an odd way of magnifying the silence. Any noise seemed a sharp contrast.

The local hardware store was a few doors down. I could probably be back in ten minutes. I asked Sarah to relay that message to any customers. They'd most likely need that long to pick something anyway. It shouldn't inconvenience anyone to wait. I didn't make it to the front door before it opened.

The familiar old man who entered was wearing at least three shirts. It was June, but the morning had been chilly. It was possible only two of his layers had long sleeves. I saw two unbuttoned cuffs and what looked like a plain T-shirt collar underneath the ones that were crooked.

He saw me and dipped into a formal bow.

"Hi, Uncle Jojo." He was technically my great-uncle.

He turned and bowed to Sarah, too.

"Hi, Jojo," she said. "How's your day so far?"

He smiled in answer, then quickly walked past me farther into the shop. He usually came in only to say hello, but it appeared this would be a longer visit. Jojo was most animated talking about food so I asked if he'd had lunch yet, even though it was a bit early for that. He made no response to my question before he ran one hand over the new patch of drywall. Then he turned and shrugged at me.

"We moved the entrance to the outside. Remember? Now we can rent the upstairs to someone who won't have to come through the shop."

I thought I saw recognition in his eyes, but he made no gestures. He communicated in such limited ways, I never knew how much he understood. After a few quiet moments, he rubbed his hand on the unpainted part and shrugged at me again.

"Yeah, it still needs paint. I was about to go get some. Do you want to come with me to the hardware store?"

His eyes widened with interest for a second. But then he shook his head, rubbed his hand over the wall and shrugged at me again.

"There's a door to the upstairs on the outside now," I explained again. "Did you see it? Simon Donnelly is going to live there. Do you know Simon?"

Jojo nodded and gave a thumbs up.

I guessed I could add him to the list of people who approved of my new tenant, not that I was a landlord.

Then Jojo turned enough to rub both hands against the wall before he faced me and shrugged bigger than ever.

I was running out of answers and began to fear he was trying to ask about Granny. He'd been inconsolable when he first learned of her death. Surely he understood that his sister was gone. I asked God for help and received some possible inspiration. Jojo had spent a lot of time visiting Granny. "Did you leave something in her apartment?" I asked.

Jojo had stopped paying attention and was halfway to the exit. "See you later, Uncle Jojo," I called after him. It was not unusual for him to abandon conversations abruptly – even mid-sentence abruptly – so I took no offense. I made a mental note to try to ask him again later and get my mom to check for things that might belong to him.

I returned to my task of getting paint, letting Sarah know I'd be back as soon as possible. The small-town hardware store didn't have a ton of options, but they had the small can of white I needed. And I remembered to buy a paintbrush, too. The friendly guy behind the counter put the can in a shaking machine for me so it'd be ready to use.

I was hit with the scent of plaster as I re-entered Granny's Shelf. I found something to prop the front door, thinking a bit of ventilation would be a good idea since I was about to add paint fumes to the air.

Sarah smiled at my common sense, and the open door might have been the invitation to a young family that entered a minute later. Two elementary-aged girls oohed and aahed at a few of the sparkling items on the front shelves before their parents steered them towards a pair of touristy souvenirs with resin lighthouses. I completed the sale before I popped open the can of paint.

I started at the top, and it only took me about thirty seconds to notice that the new paint didn't match the old paint. I assumed that was because it was wet. It would match when it was dry. White was white. Near the bottom, I sat on the plastic stool I'd used to reach the top. Granny had been only 5'1" so she'd likely used the stool more often than I would, though my three extra inches wouldn't be a big difference.

I kicked the stool out of my way as I finished and took the brush to the bathroom to rinse it off in the sink. I didn't have a hammer handy, but I found a sturdy knickknack to tap the paint lid back into place. Then I stepped back to inspect my work. How long did paint take to dry? The section I'd painted was still totally obvious. How long before it started to blend with the old paint?

I glanced at Sarah. Her eyes quickly darted away from the wall. I decided that if we were both looking at it, it was something we could try to talk about. "It's going to look better when it dries, right?"

She gave me a little shrug. "It'll be less… shiny."

I nodded my gratitude for the observation that was completely true. The wet paint probably only looked like a different shade because it was reflecting more light. "But what should I do if it still doesn't match?" I asked. "I don't want to repaint the whole place."

Sarah gave me another tentative shrug.

I realized how whiney I sounded. And her dad had stood right there and offered to paint it for me less than an hour ago.

She was considerate enough not to remind me of that. Instead, she said, "You could find a place that does paint matching and bring them a chip of the old paint. Then you'd just have to redo the space where the door was."

I stared at the wall and tried to picture myself removing a chip of paint without doing real damage.

"Or you could paint the rest of that wall with the new paint," Sarah suggested. "I think the difference would be hardly noticeable if it stopped at the corners."

That might work. It'd be like an accent wall with a teeny tiny accent. But I still hoped it wouldn't be necessary. Those hopes gradually dimmed as I spent much of my free time that afternoon watching paint dry.

2

St. Jude's church had thick wooden doors with big iron handles. I pulled one of those doors open with a heavy mix of emotions. I had attended Mass there regularly only until I was ten. More recently, I'd come with Granny at least a half-dozen times, most often at Christmas. I was always happy to reflect fondly on my faint memories when I was with her. Now I remembered the happy nostalgia with the sadness of Granny not being with me.

I walked straight to the second pew from the front on the left. That was Granny's usual spot. Though it hurt to be there without her that first time, I already knew it would become a favorite place to think of her. She always wore a joyful expression as she belted out hymns that were occasionally off-key but always enthusiastic.

A few people approached me as I was leaving to share condolences. One guy I recognized from the funeral home. The others didn't seem familiar. Yet. I stuck out as a newcomer in the small town. But I was staying. I'd figure out some names and connections eventually. I grabbed a bulletin by the exit. Maybe something in there would help me start to belong.

I didn't open the bulletin until I was sitting at my kitchen table with my lunch. I ate more yogurt than I wanted because I was trying to make everything in my fridge fit in the one cooler I owned. I did find something encouraging while I was eating. St. Jude's had a young adult group that met on Friday evenings. The notice said it was for people in their 20s and 30s. I hoped I wouldn't be the youngest one there as I put it on my calendar.

Eating the yogurt straight from the container meant I only had to wash a spoon when I was finished. It was the last thing to be added to a box. At least, I thought it was. I really didn't have a ton of stuff, but it still took almost three hours to get it all into the truck. And I kept finding loose items I needed to stuff in boxes. I rechecked the back of all the drawers and cupboards while my brother David threatened to return the U-Haul with all my stuff in it if I checked anything a third time.

I had to stop at the rental office to return my key. That was faster and smoother than I expected, which made David a bit happier. I followed the truck as I drove to Andauk the second time that day. I'd considered that Mass at my church in Pinebury would save time. But going back to St. Jude's was one of the most exciting parts of the move. And there was something unsettling about squeezing God into my day. I didn't have to, but I wanted to give him the extra time of that drive.

Watching the truck in front of me, I attempted a philosophical exercise of wondering how well I could handle the loss of all my belongings gathered into that one space. My mom and my brother were also in that truck though. I couldn't really get my head into the exercise.

13

My new apartment was in the middle of the town. We made several turns down small streets. It was a lovely afternoon, and we passed a few people doing yardwork, walking dogs, riding bikes. It looked like summer.

I waited for David to back the U-Haul onto the front yard – Mr. Franks had told my mom we should do that – before I pulled forward to park in front of the house. I could see by the address numbers that I was renting the left side of the duplex. I heard the rumble of the back of the truck sliding open as I took the steps to the porch. David was in a hurry to get unloaded. I wanted to walk through the place first so I'd have a better idea where to put the boxes.

David followed me in carrying a box.

"I need to see the layout first," I said.

"It says kitchen," he said without slowing his steps. "I think I can identify the kitchen."

He was right. We weren't trying to sort by conservatory, morning room and parlor. I had a basic kitchen, living room, bedroom and bathroom, all connected to each other. Most of my things were labeled or easily identified by those categories. "You're right," I admitted. "It's best to get the truck unloaded quickly and leave me to organize by myself."

He smiled at my concession. "Glad you figured out what has been the plan all along."

I did take a quick peek in each room before heading back outside. The kitchen was tiny but had an extra wide window over the sink. The bedroom closet had doors that seemed tricky to keep on the tracks. The living room had a ceiling fan. There was a new

14

carpet odor throughout the place, which I preferred to wondering how old the carpet was.

I passed David coming in with his second box as I went out to grab my first. Mom was standing on the porch typing something on her phone. Two boys who looked about twelve or thirteen had stopped their bikes in the middle of the street to watch. I almost hoped we dropped something. The parade of furniture wouldn't be much entertainment otherwise.

When I came out of the house next, there was a guy about my age standing on my porch. "Hi," he said. "Are you Cassidy?"

That was a super easy question I stumbled over. I didn't know where he came from, and he smiled at me hopefully as he asked. Something about his appearance made my stomach jump as though maybe it loved all that yogurt after all. "Uh… yeah," I said.

"Great." He held out his hand. "I'm Jackson. My mom told me you were moving in today so I'm here to offer my services."

I shook his hand, and he kept talking before I could say anything else.

"By services, I mean my hands. I can't guarantee I won't drop anything, but I'll try not to."

Those boys were still watching. I couldn't help wondering if we'd shared a thought about giving them a show. What I wondered more was who his mom was and how she knew about me moving in.

"You're here to help?" My mom was more or less between us with her hand on the guy's shoulder, already steering him towards the truck. "That's my son David over there who would rather risk dropping the washing machine off the back of the truck than let his old, frail mom help him get it on the dolly. Please give him a hand."

15

"I'm on it." Jackson jogged down the steps with a glance back at me that said he was amused at being put to work so quickly.

When I was sure he was out of earshot, I leaned closer to my mom. "Do you know who that is?"

"Didn't he just introduce himself to you?"

"He only told me his first name," I said. "How did he know who I was? And where did he come from?" The only other car on the street had been there when we arrived.

"He knew who you were?"

"Yeah."

Mom considered for a moment and then shrugged. "Doesn't matter. Looks like he can be useful." She nodded at the washing machine coming down the ramp without incident. "And he's cute."

I'd noticed that, which was why I tried not to blush when Mom pointed it out. I rushed off to get something to carry when I knew my effort was unsuccessful. I hadn't decided what I should grab next when Mr. Franks arrived.

"Hey, Miss Bodner," he said. "Looks like you found the place all right."

"Yeah. It looks good."

"We'll talk more before I leave." He kept moving towards the house – hadn't fully stopped as he greeted me – and called out, "You boys know how to hook that up?"

David had taken pictures of the back of the washing machine before he unhooked it so he'd be able to set it up at the new place. It sounded, however, as though Mr. Franks already knew what to do and wanted to help. He was even carrying a toolbox. I hadn't noticed from which direction he'd approached the back of the

16

truck. I saw no new cars as I stepped out with a box. I guessed all of my neighbors were just popping in out of thin air.

My mom caught up to me. "I bet we can get that table in before they come back for the dryer."

"Don't want David to see you carrying it?" I asked.

"Just want to make sure he's too late to stop me," she said. "Honestly, I'm fifty-one, not ninety-one. Did he think I was coming to watch?"

The kitchen table only sat four people. It was light enough I could have carried it myself. I set my box on top to make it more challenging for the two of us.

The laundry hookups were basically part of the kitchen, though a door slid in front of them. I was glad I heard Mr. Franks' voice before we entered. Otherwise, I might not have known the older man sprawled on the floor was fine. He was explaining to David and Jackson how to make sure the machine was level. That step probably wasn't in David's pictures.

Jackson smiled at me as I set the table down on the far side of the room. Given the size of the room, the far side was barely past Mr. Franks' feet.

"I'm glad you have someone with real services to offer," Jackson said, nodding towards the floor.

My hair was in a high ponytail that I braided to keep neat and out of the way. I ran my hand down the length of it to be sure it was still smooth.

Jackson started to say something else, but a loud groan filled the room as Mr. Franks pulled himself to standing.

"Hot water's on the left," he said. "Let's see if you can hook it up."

David leaned in quickly, eager to learn.

"Doesn't look like I'm needed here," Jackson said. "I'll follow you out for another load." He looked at me for approval.

My hand reached back and smoothed my braid again before I realized he'd said he'd *follow* me. Because I was supposed to be getting something else, too. "Right," I said. "There is still quite a bit in the truck."

I caught my mom suppressing a smirk as I made my way back out the front door. She was using her phone again and didn't come outside with us.

"That's your mom, right?" Jackson gestured back towards the kitchen.

I nodded and considered asking about his mom. It seemed weird now that he hadn't just mentioned her. He barely paused long enough for me to think about it anyway.

"Is she... Was Mrs. Johnson your mom's mom?"

The question sounded as though he was merely confirming something he already knew. How much did this guy know about me? I nodded again to keep him talking.

"Is she going to help you run Granny's Shelf?"

"No. That'll just be me."

"Cool. When we heard Mrs. Johnson passed, people wondered if the store would close, and..." Jackson stopped at the back of the U-Haul, talking and walking. He turned to face me. "I'm sorry. I shouldn't be talking about your grandma without first saying I'm sorry she's gone. I didn't really know her well, but... I'm still sorry."

"Thank you." Hearing people say the same words over and over was comforting in this case. Granny lived a good life and even

18

people who didn't know her personally knew she'd be missed. The evidence of a legacy lifted my spirits.

"What should I get next?" He skipped the ramp to jump into the back. "How about the mattress? But the box springs should go first, right? Or... wait... is that the base? The frame? What do you call the part that holds the bed up, and are those pieces it?"

"Uh, yeah." I only answered one question because he seemed to be thinking out loud more than asking me anything.

"Okay. Maybe if I carry in the mattress and the box springs and just set them up against a wall in the bedroom, maybe you can get the frame thing put together by the time I get both inside, and then I'll help you get everything stacked up."

"I'll try," I said. I climbed up next to him and bent to gather up the frame parts.

"That wasn't meant to be a challenge. Like, see if you can do that by the time I do this. I just thought it might be about the same... the frame probably takes longer. I don't even know how to... Anyway, take your time."

I didn't want to take my time. I wanted to grab all four parts with perfect coordination and jump gracefully out of the truck, then set the frame up before he even got the box springs inside. Instead, I tried to pick up the head and footboards by the middles. One tipped to my right and the other tipped to my left, and I only barely managed not to hit myself in the face with either. After a minute of repositioning, I got them both tucked under one arm. Then I squatted to grab both side supports at one end. I figured I could drag the other ends rather than try to balance anything else. That worked, except that it made an awful scraping noise as I

19

walked down the ramp. I sent an apologetic glance over my shoulder.

Jackson beamed at my accomplishment and turned to start tugging on the mattress.

I snagged the tail end of the sides on one of the steps getting onto the porch. I stumbled, but I did not fall down or drop anything. Thankfully, I also did not look back to see if anyone had seen.

Water was flowing into my washing machine as I passed, which was progress. I stood in the bedroom doorway while I decided which wall the bed should go against. I leaned the headboard there, tossed the footboard to the side and got on my knees to slide the side into place. I hadn't given up on the challenge that wasn't a challenge.

The mattress appeared in the doorway. I recognized Jackson's khaki shorts and bright sneakers under it. He seemed to be struggling only with the awkward size and not the weight. He was skinny but still strong. He set it against the opposite wall. "I did not knock your mom over with that," he said, "so, um…" He finished with a thumbs up and left the room, leaving me wondering how close he'd come to doing that.

I laughed to myself as I resumed my task. The sides had cross supports I unfolded before scrambling to retrieve the footboard. I snapped that into place and stood up just as Jackson returned. He was behind the box springs, which was great. That meant he couldn't see me grinning stupidly at him. I inhaled a bit of nonchalance and told him the frame was ready.

He tipped a corner to the floor and pivoted to look around his load. "The timing did work out." He sounded impressed, but I couldn't tell if he noticed my speed or was only congratulating himself on predicting correctly.

I ran my hand down my braid again. I needed to stop doing that before he thought it was a nervous habit. Or worse, he might think *he* made me nervous. "I'll get something else," I said, rushing from the room. I considered that I could have helped him stack the bed. But if he could carry the heavy parts all the way from the truck, he could set them on the frame by himself. That was sound reasoning. It was mostly an embarrassing mental picture of me trying to help and getting somehow squished between the mattress and the wall that kept my feet moving towards a different task.

I stopped at the base of the ramp and waved to those two boys with their bikes. One raised a hand in a gesture that almost counted as a return wave before they both took off. All my help was still in the house. I had a moment of feeling small and alone as I watched the boys pedal away. It wasn't a sad moment because I knew I wasn't truly alone. I smiled at the idea that I might have scared the boys into thinking I'd ask if they wanted to help.

"Cassidy!" Jackson called to me as he bounded off my porch. "Mr. Franks needs to leave soon, and he wants to show you some important things before he does." He gave emphasis to the words important things as though he thought that a strange request.

"What important things?" I asked.

He continued to walk towards me, or rather my furniture he was helping to move, with an expression that suggested he wanted a witty answer and was unable to think of one.

I pressed the question with silence.

Jackson stopped with one hand on the side of the truck, ready to hop inside again. He glanced back with a wince. "Okay, fine. I have no idea what you need to know, and I'm very curious. I hope you can tell me about some of it later." He appeared to fight a smile and some nerves about admitting he'd like to talk to me more. Both worked to make me suddenly less nervous around him.

"Now I'm curious," I said. "I guess I better find out some important stuff." I headed back to the house. I got halfway there before I realized I could have carried something. I didn't have a lot of practice moving, and I was distracted by trying to figure out something else that could be important.

I'd only thought of three women in town who knew enough about me and what day I was moving into town that they could be Jackson's mom. One of them was Mrs. Franks, who would have heard plenty from Sarah. But Jackson probably would not have referred to his dad as Mr. Franks. That ruled her out. My other guesses were Mrs. Sweet, who seemed around my mom's age and had mentioned a son, and Mrs. Donnelly, because I knew Simon had at least one brother.

Mr. Franks was eager to begin what he called my grand tour. He pointed out the fuse box and the main water valve. He showed me how to lean into the closet door to keep it on the track. He talked about how he'd put in new carpet because the previous occupant had a dog and how he might need to raise his pet fee. He demonstrated how the loose shower knob still worked and what to do if it fell off. He assured me he'd get a replacement for that as soon as he found the right one. And he pointed out a few things that he'd fixed for me.

Despite a few remaining flaws, I had no doubt I was getting a good deal on the apartment. Mr. Franks made sure I had his number before he left. He had seemed certain that something would come up to make me need it, and yet that didn't worry me because he'd also seemed perfectly capable of handling whatever that might be. He was a better landlord than I was, not that I was calling myself a landlord.

3

By the time I finished the grand tour of my new home, quite a few boxes had been stacked around me. Mr. Franks barely got out the front door before Jackson and David blocked it trying to get my loveseat through. I could hear my mom's voice outside giving confusing instructions on which way to tip it to angle the high armrests around the doorframe. Since I wasn't going anywhere until they got out of the way, I took the opportunity to study Jackson unobserved.

I noticed he was attractive right away. I was single. Of course I wondered if there was any possibility of a romantic relationship. It seemed likely that he lived within walking distance, and a helpful friend nearby would also be valuable. I couldn't learn much about those possibilities from his appearance. I was studying him for resemblance to either of my guesses on his last name.

His most prominent feature was slightly overlarge ears. Or maybe they only stuck out from his head more than average. That seemed like a family trait, but I didn't remember seeing it on Mrs. Sweet or Mrs. Donnelly. They both had longer hair that might have covered it though. Simon's ears weren't as prominent. Jackson's hair was very short on the sides and back. It was long enough on top to better show the color. I was struck by how similar it was to the wood grain on the end of the loveseat he was trying to turn the way my mom suggested while she yelled at David to lift his end higher. Most people would simply describe the color as light brown. But both the hair and the wood had streaks of various shades, highlights and lowlights. God colored more masterfully than someone with a crayon. I tore my thoughts from the mystery of the Great Designer to my earthly mystery.

Jackson had freckles across his nose and under his eyes. Mrs. Sweet wore a coat of make-up. Maybe she was covering up matching freckles. I wasn't sure I could count a possibility as a clue.

Jackson took several quick backwards steps as the puzzle of getting the loveseat through the doorway was solved. I got out of the way and out of my head.

"Where do you want this?" David asked.

"Uh... that wall."

Jackson tried to move the way I pointed, but David held his end steady. His face showed annoyance. "Is that actually where you want it, or are you having us put it somewhere close to be nice and then you're going to move it by yourself later?"

It had been a long day if my being nice was irritating. "I don't know where I want it," I admitted. "Isn't it better to have you put it down rather than hold it while I decide? That might take days."

"Yes, thank you," Jackson said.

David rolled his eyes and caused Jackson to stumble with a sudden step towards that wall. Fortunately, no one fell or got crushed by the furniture.

My mom had her phone out again. "I'm going to take a few pictures of the place to show Ava."

I nodded. Pictures might be the only way my sister would see where I lived. That melancholy thought had me staring into space for a moment. When I realized the guys were headed out for another load, I made a move to follow them.

Jackson stopped me at the door. "It's getting late, Cassidy. You can start unpacking while we get the rest off the truck. Otherwise, you might not have the place livable at a decent hour."

I glanced at David, who had stopped on the porch. He gave a small nod of concession. It was after seven, and I had promised him pizza in exchange for helping. I guessed that explained some crankiness. "I'll order dinner, too," I said. "Is everyone okay with pepperoni?"

David nodded as he walked away, and Jackson said that sounded delicious.

I turned around and almost collided with my mom. She let the guys get a bit farther away before leaning even closer. "He's cute *and* considerate." Then she held up a picture of Jackson on her phone. "I got a good one while capturing the layout. I'll send it to you in case you want to ask anyone in town about him."

"I'm not going to do that, Mom," I said. Though I hoped that wouldn't stop her from sending me the picture.

She shrugged and followed the guys outside.

I went into the bedroom to order a couple of pizzas while I thought about what needed to happen to make the place livable in time to get enough sleep. The thought of sleep made getting sheets on the bed a logical starting point. I found the sheets as soon as dinner was on the way. I only had to look in two boxes. I'd started hanging up some clothes when Jackson came in with a floor lamp.

"Do you want this in here or the living room?" he asked.

"How do you know I don't want it right in the middle of the bathroom?"

"I'll put it there if you want." He sounded playfully threatening.

We shared a brief chuckle over the idea before I told him he could leave it in the nearest corner.

"You need to think about where to put the lamp for a few days, too?"

I could tell he was referring to the earlier discussion, but he paused as he set the lamp down. There appeared to be interest, if I wanted to talk about it. Genuine interest in my thoughts on where to put a lamp? That better not be an act because I was starting to like Jackson.

"I... well, I bought it for the bedroom in my old apartment because there was no overhead light. There is one here."

"Oh, so you do actually need to live here – or at least spend time in the dark – before you figure out where you want more light."

"Yes." The understanding made us both smile. I guessed I wasn't smiling too much if I wasn't smiling more than him.

"That's a pretty dress," he said.

I had changed from my church clothes to casual shorts. He meant the dress I was hanging up. It had light blue lace over a darker blue layer and was one of my favorites, too. "Thank you."

"So I know Mrs. Johnson was her brother's guardian. Is your mom taking care of Jojo now?" Jackson fidgeted as he moved

27

closer. He was no longer standing in the corner by the lamp. "I just wonder if he has to move or some other big change."

"I don't know. Well, he doesn't have to move." I put down the hanger I'd picked up. Jojo was a subject too complicated to multitask. "If there are any big changes, that'll probably mean I've done something wrong."

"Oh. Are you..." He hesitated, clearly wanting to ask but only if I wanted to answer.

I nodded at everything he didn't say. "I'm his legal guardian now."

"Did your grandma talk to you about that before or... I, uh... you seem not totally comfortable about it or something."

"No, she asked me. Sort of. She did, but..." If he hadn't already picked up on my cluelessness, the lack of coherence would have tipped him off. I took a breath and tried again. "Granny asked me when I was nineteen. She told me he mostly takes care of himself and just needs someone to handle the financial stuff and that she'd leave me good instructions for all that. She was mostly concerned about the legal paperwork, wanted to have that in order. She thought it'd be easier on everyone if it was decided ahead of time who would be named guardian.

"She asked me like there wasn't a single doubt in her head that I was capable of stepping into her huge shoes. I think it was a combination of me being too flattered to disappoint her and me thinking Uncle Jojo would probably die first, even though he's ten years younger than her, or that I'd be at least thirty before it happened and therefore magically twice as smart and capable as I am now. Anyway, I just agreed without asking many questions."

"What do you wish you'd asked?"

28

"I don't know, and that's the real problem," I said. "I feel so bad that I never gave it enough thought to know what I should have asked. I keep thinking about... There was one time someone called the police because he thought Jojo stole something and... I guess he did steal it, but the other guy didn't know that Jojo didn't know what he was doing exactly. He didn't understand it belonged to someone. Granny gave it back and smoothed everything over, and I don't have any idea how she did that. And what if... what if Jojo got hurt or has some medical emergency? I think I'd be supposed to do something."

"Your lawyer could help with something like that, right?"

"Uh... yeah." I was momentarily thrown by the odd inflection of his question. It kind of sounded as though he was afraid of offending my lawyer, who was not in earshot, and also kind of afraid he wasn't even sure he should know I had a lawyer. I guessed he was trying to ask if I did. The distraction of that worked to dispel the panic I was generating. "She's super nice and said I could call her anytime. I need to remember not to be anxious and worried about many things when there is need of only one thing."

"Mary has chosen the better part," he said as he recognized my quote.

It hadn't been a test, but I still found myself relieved that Jackson knew something of the Bible. If he was faithful, that could help us become good friends.

"Still," he continued, "a big responsibility can... a little concern doesn't have to mean needless anxiety. Have you worked out the day to day of his needs?"

"Yeah. Granny did leave great instructions on… everything. She wrote everything down. Do you know Jojo?" I wanted to turn the conversation because I was suddenly embarrassed about how much we were talking about me.

"It's a small town. It'd be hard not to know who he is. I mostly know him from… he comes into Pans and Plates sometimes. We're supposed to watch and make a note whenever he takes a plate home so we can let Mrs. Johnson know how many to find and bring back."

"We?" Pans and Plates was the local pizza place. The place I'd called for dinner. "Do you work there?"

"Oh, yeah. I didn't tell you that, did I? I've only been there about a month, but I love it except… uh… it annoys my parents."

"They have some sort of feud with the owners?"

"No, it's just… They're not really upset with me or anything." He paused for a moment to emphasize the point that he wasn't talking about serious tension. "I finished college in May and my parents are like four years of school to make pizza? Exaggerated sigh."

I laughed at his impression. "I assume that means you didn't get a degree in pizza so…"

He nodded at my prompt. "Accounting."

"Are you looking for something in that field?"

"No. Not anymore. Or maybe just not right now. I, uh… Do you want my life story?"

"Sure." I tried to match his joking tone. It sounded as though he was worried about talking too much, and I wanted to reassure him without sounding overly interested in his life story.

Even though I was very interested. I resumed hanging up clothes to present a casual front to my listening.

"I majored in accounting because I've always liked math and thought working with numbers would be a good job. But then last summer I worked at an accounting place and... everyone there was so stressed out all the time and I lost count of the number of times I heard someone say, 'At least it's not tax season.' Every time someone said it, I was like *it gets worse?* And it might have only been that one place, but it was enough to make me rethink my career plans. I had no idea what else I might want to do. I thought it was a good idea to finish the degree since I only had one year left, and any degree might make my resume slightly more respectable for whatever... I, uh, I had a generous scholarship so it didn't cost much. Anyway, I still didn't know what to do when I graduated. I had submitted a resume to several office-type places, places that seemed like maybe a college grad would... I even got two offers. One would have been a long drive and neither felt like a good fit. Meanwhile, I know the family that runs Pans and Plates. No feud," he flashed a smile, "and they were really needing some help. I decided to go where I felt needed."

"Who doesn't relate to that feeling?" I asked.

"Exactly. My parents mostly get it. I mean, I live with them, and they're not threatening to kick me out or anything. My dad still thinks I should come work with him though. He sells insurance and my sister plans to quit soon because she's expecting her first kid. But she's already training someone and..."

Jackson's last few words were coated with a light scraping sound which caused us to look to the corner just in time to see the lamp sliding down the wall as it tipped towards the floor. He

31

lunged to grab it. He wasn't fast enough. Between the carpet and it being fairly lightweight, there wasn't much of a crash, more of a shudder. The shade popped off and began to roll in a circle. Jackson chased it while he apologized. "I'm sorry. It felt wobbly when I set it down, but when it didn't fall right away, I figured it was stable enough."

It took him a few tries to grab that lamp shade. Watching him spin as it rolled in tighter circles was a tiny bit amusing, only a tiny bit. It should have made me smile, and that's it. But I didn't want him to think I was laughing at him so I tried to fight it. The harder I tried to fight it, the more it fought back. My hint of a smile turned into a full laugh. And I tried to fight that, too.

Jackson looked at me pinching my lips and shaking. He narrowed his eyes and said, "Glad you're not upset."

I relaxed enough to laugh and be done with it. "I should have mentioned it's fallen down before," I said. "But it did look stable when… I thought the corner had it propped up."

He set the lamp upright and slid the shade over the bulb. Then he stood with his hands poised to catch it. He made a few sudden jerks even though the lamp didn't move. His attempt to make me laugh was working.

But David walked in to interrupt. "I don't think that pizza is ever going to get here so I'm just going to take the truck through a drive-through on my way back."

My mom came in on his heels. Her hands were popping up and down at her sides as though she was trying to refrain from grabbing him.

I checked the time and realized it had been almost an hour since I ordered the pizza. I said, "The truck is empty?"

David rolled his eyes. "For a while now."

His reaction made me feel several steps behind everyone else. Jackson pulled his phone from his pocket as he volunteered to check on the pizza. I lowered my eyes to the box of clothes while I processed the situation. As eager as Jackson was to help, I could probably assume that lamp was the last thing off the truck. My mom hovering behind David likely meant she'd kept him in the other room as long as she could. I wondered if Jackson knew she'd been intentionally giving him time to talk to me. And I wondered if he'd consider it a good thing if he did know. I'd been talking about some fairly personal stuff with a guy who might have been humoring me while he waited for free food.

I was too distracted by trying to decide how embarrassed to be – and my mom looking at me like I should have news to share was tipping the needle higher – to hear what Jackson said on the phone. But I could tell the tone was friendly and not at all like a complaining customer so I was happy he made the call.

He looked at all of us as he hung up and said, "Someone messed up the delivery order and let yours get cold so they had to redo it. But it still should have been here by... I bet that's it." Someone knocked while he was talking.

I answered the door because it was my door, though the foreign layout hadn't convinced me of that yet. The man with the pizza had barely greeted me before he noticed Jackson – whom he clearly knew – standing over my shoulder. Jackson explained that he'd been about to explain to me that I'd already been refunded for the pizza because of the mistake. He took the boxes, and the man apologized again, wished me a good evening, and jogged back towards his waiting car. At least someone in town arrived by predictable means.

When I closed the door, two pizzas were sitting on my kitchen table and three guests were looking at me expectantly. "Here's napkins," I said as I grabbed a roll of paper towels, which was basically the same as napkins. "I can find plates if you want to give me a minute."

David shook his head and Jackson said, "Not necessary."

My mom appeared mildly dismayed at my hostess skills but did not insist I find plates. She folded her hands. We mirrored each other in a Sign of the Cross to begin the blessing. Jackson joined in as though it was second nature. I resisted some giddiness at another point in his favor.

David flipped open a box and helped himself to the first slice of pizza. Jackson ripped off napkins and handed one to everyone before he picked up a slice. He did not immediately take a bite. "I'm going to take mine to go," he said, "so I can get out of your way while you unpack. Thanks for letting me help today."

I had already opened my mouth to thank him, but the words wouldn't come out after he thanked me for the same thing. I must have looked as though I was gaping at him in my confusion.

He paused by the door. "St. Jude's young adult group meets Fridays at seven. You should totally come and meet some great people."

"Yeah. I, uh... I saw that in the bulletin."

"Good. I'll look for you." His eyes swept over David and my mom as he said it was nice to meet all of us. Then he backed out the door saluting us with a slice of pizza.

"I like him," my mom said.

34

I looked to make sure the door was fully closed.

"He's too nice," David said through a mouthful. "It's an act for Cassidy's sake."

I felt my brother was wrong, yet I also felt disappointed at the idea that Jackson was just nice to everyone. I picked up a slice of pizza – the delicious scent made my stomach rumble – without commenting on either observation.

It was fortunate that my mom was only hungry enough for one slice. David had downed three and was urging her to leave before she'd even finished her first. They both gave me quick hugs on their way out. My mom's was an overly tight squeeze while my brother's was more of a pat on the back from the front.

I finished my dinner in contemplative silence. There was so much I had to do, but I refused to be overwhelmed by it. Feeding myself was important, too. I was allowed to enjoy some nourishment while I made a mental list of what I could reasonably accomplish before calling it a night. It was spectacularly good pizza, which made it easier than I expected to delay the waiting tasks.

I slid the leftovers into the fridge, happy that I had at least one easy meal in my future. Then I set about the most basic organization. I found everything that was necessary for day-to-day functioning and that included having the cards and pictures for a prayer corner in my bedroom. I set my heavily bookmarked journal on top of my Bible on the pretty little table. With my sanctuary inside my sanctuary ready, I could finally get some sleep. But I made the mistake of checking for messages first. There was a text from my dad. He asked if we could get together some time to talk.

35

I set the phone down in the kitchen and walked away from it. I could still see the message in my head as I began several hours of tossing and turning. I knew Dad had my number. He'd been in touch with Ava, and she gave it to him. I had spent so much time trying to think what I would say if he called me, what I wanted to say and what I needed to say. I hadn't come up with good answers before Granny died. Everything after that happened so fast that Dad got pushed to the back of my mind with a mix of relief and disappointment that he might have changed his mind about trying to reconnect.

My dad picked a lousy time to insert himself onto my chore list. I knew that wasn't his fault. More than anything, I didn't want talking to my dad to feel like a chore. There was nothing I could do about that.

4

$\mathscr{G}$ranny's Shelf generally did the most business on Saturdays so Granny gave herself Sunday and Monday off. I woke up that Monday with swirling thoughts and emotions that didn't exactly coincide with the idea of a vacation day. I wrote down my most dominant concerns. I stared at the Divine Mercy image as I tried to give it all to God for him to give back to me one task at a time. I moved on to breakfast knowing that Jojo was my first priority of the day.

Granny had an entire bin of journals regarding her brother. She kept journals about everything. She encouraged me to read some even while she was still alive. My favorites were the oldest, the ones with stories about her learning to be a wife and mother. I used to ask her questions and get her to share more details. We talked about marriage most when I was in high school. I was confused that I wanted what hadn't worked well for my parents, and it helped to hear of Granny's success. My mom had most of the journals now, but I had the ones about Jojo.

I knew I'd find a few funny anecdotes, but most of the content was more practical. Granny kept records of all the errands she ran on his behalf and the chores she did. She wrote down things other people said about him when she thought it might be useful to engage him in conversation. She described signs he used in case they became consistent, things that seemed to make him smile and things he didn't seem to remember. I studied the most recent entries until I had my list ready. It was the first page of a new notebook I bought for my own records.

I had time to unpack a few boxes. Later I would need to stop at the local grocery store to pay Jojo's bill. He didn't have anything due at the library. On the way to Jojo's place, I'd need to ask at Pans and Plates if he had any of their plates and also ask what those plates looked like so I'd know them if I saw them. That made me wonder briefly if I'd see Jackson there. I guessed it was brief. I didn't set a timer for how long I thought about that.

All my errands needed to be wrapped up by 3 o'clock. That's what time I was meeting Simon Donnelly. I was supposed to be there in case he had any questions as he moved in. I didn't know if I'd be able to answer any questions. I also didn't know if I could paint a wall in the same amount of time and whether or not I could do that without him asking me why I was painting a white wall white.

Before I could execute my fabulous plan for the day, I needed to address that sleep-stealing text from my dad. I replied that I needed time to think about whether or not I wanted to see him. It felt mean. But it was also honest. If he really wanted to know me, he needed to accept my honesty.

The grocery store was easy. I picked up a few items to stock my new kitchen and the man behind the deli counter somehow knew I was Evelyn Johnson's granddaughter and why I was there before I introduced myself. Pans and Plates was at the end of Main

Street. I guessed it wasn't really the end, but it was on a corner and the last business before the houses started.

I used my business-owner privilege of a free parking space behind Granny's Shelf. There were three of them. Simon would get one with his rent. Sarah lived across the street and ran back and forth to her greenhouse. She wouldn't need that other space. I prayed that someday I'd have a husband who might park there. He might stop in to have lunch with me or maybe to surprise me with some flowers for my birthday.

The idyllic fantasy was interrupted by thoughts that Sarah sold flowers. It wouldn't be much of a surprise if I saw him buying some from her, and there was the fact that I had no mental picture of this make-believe future husband anyway. Back in reality, I was facing the door to the pizza place. A guy with a stack of boxes came out and held the door open for me with his foot.

The floor was black-and-white checkerboard tiles. I looked up from that and recognized the man who had delivered my pizza standing behind the counter. He was on the phone but nodded politely at me. I could see a few people working behind him. Jackson wasn't one of them.

"Hello!" The man greeted me cheerfully as he hung up the phone. "Have you forgiven us for the late pizza?"

"I… uh…" The question took me by surprise because I'd mostly forgotten it had been late, and I didn't know if he'd recognize me. "Yes," I said. "I'm not here for pizza right now though. I'm supposed to talk to Dan about Jojo."

"Well, I'm Dan. What about Jojo?"

"I'm supposed to ask if he has any of your plates."

"Oh!" Understanding caused a smile to bloom across his face. "You must be Evelyn's granddaughter. I hadn't made the connection."

The smile eased my nerves. I told myself that the people on my list were more accustomed to my rather unusual errands than I was. "I am," I said. "Her notes said you'd expect me on Mondays."

He nodded. "She was a sweet old lady. I was sorry to hear about her passing. Also very glad to meet a young woman willing to step into all the responsibility she had."

"Thanks." I hoped he realized that was about his condolences and not bragging about being super responsible. And then I spotted the hint about meeting me. "I'm Cassidy Bodner, by the way."

"Dan Farwin, as you probably know from those notes." He smiled again before turning more thoughtful. "I haven't seen Jojo for a few days, but since no one was here to ask about plates last week he probably has at least one." Dan bent to look at something under the counter. "Yep. Three."

"Okay. Can you show me one of your plates so I know what I'm looking for?"

"Hey! You're new. Try this." A younger guy – I guessed still in his twenties – had jogged up from the back. He reached a fork across the counter as he spoke. There was a bite of what looked like pizza on the end of it.

"Noah!" Dan had a chastising tone as he put a hand on the new guy's forearm to pull it back. "You can't go around randomly waving forks in people's faces."

40

"It's a clean fork," Noah said, to Dan and to me. "She needs to try it while it's still warm." His eyes continued to bounce between us with a plaintive expression.

"My son is on a perpetual quest to improve what doesn't need improvement." Dan's explanation also presented the question of whether or not I was willing to participate in this quest.

I held my hand out to accept the fork.

Noah appeared grateful as I popped the bite into my mouth, and he watched closely for my reaction.

I tasted pepperoni. If my memory was accurate, it tasted very much like the pepperoni pizza I'd had for dinner. It was delicious, but I didn't know what to say because I didn't detect anything different, let alone better or worse.

"It's good, right?" Noah prompted.

I nodded. There was no arguing with that simple adjective.

"But it isn't *better*," Dan said.

"Wait. Have you tried our pizza?" Noah asked.

"Yeah. It's good."

Dan gestured to me as though I'd just proven his point.

I wasn't sure what his point was or how I'd helped it by agreeing with both of them.

"There was pepperoni in your bite," Noah said.

And now I was really confused because it sounded as though he was trying to tell me exactly how that bite was better than the pizza I'd eaten with pepperoni.

"Oh, look. Now she's speechless," Dan said.

"Because of my brilliance."

"Because she doesn't know how to tell you it tastes exactly the same."

41

My curiosity grew as I relaxed. It was becoming clear this was a long-standing argument I had little power to affect. "What was different?" I asked Noah.

"Ha!" Dan gave a gloating laugh and gestured again to me being on his side.

I was kind of leaning that way.

Noah was undaunted. "I cut up the pepperoni," he said. "When it's in quarters instead of big circles, it spreads out to every bite better. Plus, it looks nicer. The visual appeal adds to the flavor enhancement, and you know what... I bet you need a whole slice to appreciate the effect."

I started to agree. I barely dipped my chin before I cut it off. He might have a valid point, but I didn't want anyone to think I was asking for a free slice of pizza. I already had free pizza in my fridge for a mistake I didn't think warranted it.

"Even if being able to spread out the pepperoni a tiny bit more created a tiny, tiny flavor enhancement," Dan paused to roll his eyes as he put air quotes around the last two words, "it would not be nearly enough to make up for all the time it would take us to cut up the pepperoni. How long did that one take you?"

"Not long," Noah said. "I'm good with a knife."

Dan sighed audibly. "It also would not make up for the added risk to people who think they are good with knives."

Noah opened his mouth to protest, but his dad cut him off.

"Just show her the plate the slice is on."

Noah's eyes crinkled in confusion.

I shared the sentiment for a brief moment. I was so entertained by the squabbling, I'd forgotten why I was there.

Dan explained as Noah turned around to grab a plate. "Cassidy here is Evelyn Johnson's granddaughter. She'll be collecting plates for Jojo now."

Noah nodded at the introduction as I took note of the plate he held up. It was a red circle of hard plastic and seemed easy to identify because I knew Jojo's plates were white. I reminded myself I'd be looking for three of them. Then I told both guys it'd been nice to meet them, which was absolutely true, and I retreated out the front door.

****

I had been to Jojo's place with Granny a few times. The last visit wasn't very recent. Anxiety crept up to me on the sidewalk. It whispered scenarios where Jojo wept because my presence reminded him his sister was no longer alive. It suggested he might be upset that I did the chores differently. It gave me an advance feeling of the frustration I'd endure if I couldn't understand his requests.

I paused in front of the door. It was a wide porch with a door to another apartment on the far side. There was stillness on that porch even as the trees behind me swished in a gentle breeze. I invited God into that stillness to be with me no matter what happened. The anxiety about what might never happen began to dissipate, and I knocked on the door. There was no answer after a second knock either. I pulled out my key. My hand shook a little as I stuck it in the lock. I guessed I would eventually get used to letting myself into my uncle's apartment.

"Jojo? Are you home?" I called out as the door opened. It was possible he had decided not to answer, and I didn't want to startle him.

The only response was extreme quiet. I set my bag on the table and pulled out my list to get to work. I opened and recycled most of the mail. Jojo brought it inside and carefully stacked it with the largest envelopes on the bottom and smallest on top. He must have reordered it every day to keep it so neat. Granny had still paid most of his bills with checks. I'd already modernized most of it with the help of her records, but I would need to keep checking the mail for anything that needed attention.

I washed the dishes in the sink and found one red plate. There were two others in the cupboard. My mom had stopped in to do some of the chores the previous Monday while I worked my final shift. I dumped the laundry basket into the washing machine. I wouldn't need to wait for the end of the cycle since Jojo liked to hang his clothes to dry. He left them hanging until he wore them. Ropes of clothes crisscrossed his bedroom for that purpose.

I looked for things to dust and ran a vacuum over the carpet. The place was actually very tidy despite a few oddities. Jojo had a small old TV that he kept on its side. Granny said that as far as she knew, he never watched anything on it but still resisted her suggestions to get rid of it. He also had a fish tank of blue water and no fish. Granny told me he'd never had a fish.

There was a dish in one corner of the living room between two perfect stacks – the labels lined up – of cat food. Jojo did not have a cat. Granny suspected that he'd been feeding one of his neighbors' cats, but she hadn't been able to figure out whose cat it was or whether or not the owner minded.

44

I didn't know how much effort I should put into solving that mystery. Granny's notes documented her feelings on the subject. She believed it was her responsibility to track down the owner and get permission on Jojo's behalf for whatever interactions he had with the cat. She didn't want any silent resentment building.

I didn't feel it needed special effort. It seemed that everyone in town knew Granny took care of Jojo – and word was quickly spreading that I'd taken over – so if no one mentioned it to either of us, it probably didn't bother anyone. Didn't most cats hunt their own food while they were out? The owner might not have even noticed if Jojo opened a can for it now and then. But I would still keep my eyes and ears open for any indication I should explain something.

Jojo didn't come home before I finished. I wrote, "Hi, Uncle Jojo," on a sticky note and left it where the mail had been. I didn't know for sure he could read. Granny thought he could but only a little bit. I hoped he at least recognized his own nickname. I drew a quick smiley face next to it, too. Then I grabbed my bag and locked up behind myself.

# 5

Simon Donnelly was an especially good-looking man. He was tall with dark hair and deep brown eyes. I wondered if he looked anything like the first man because I could totally picture God making Simon and saying, "Yeah. I did a good job there." He'd been slightly dressed up the one time I met him, khaki pants and button-front shirt, and I'd assumed he'd come straight from work.

He showed up to move in wearing a similar outfit. The shirt was a red and blue plaid that looked nice on him the way a glorious sunset looks nice in the sky. I was wearing an old orange VBS T-shirt that I'd been happy about five minutes earlier when I dripped paint on it. I was less happy standing in front of a guy who appeared to have stepped off a catalog page to unload furniture.

"Hi, Cassidy," he said. "Nice to see you again."

And he was polite, too. "Hi," I said. My brain tried to stop gaping as I scrambled for something interesting to say. The key was in my pocket and handing it over was my sole responsibility at the moment. But I worried handing it over immediately would feel as though I was trying to get rid of him. "You, uh... have any trouble fitting everything in one load?" I nodded to the rental truck behind him.

"It was closer than I expected," he said. "I actually have a pile of stuff in the cab."

I should offer to help. It was the right thing to do even when I thought this guy was like ten times as strong as me, and I was feeling super inadequate. I tried to cover my doubts with humor. "Do you want me to help? I'm sure you have some lighter boxes I could carry and save you some trips."

"Oh, no." He waved away my offer as though it was overly generous. "I don't want to put you out, and I should have some help coming any minute."

"Okay. Let me know if you change your mind." I pulled the key from my pocket. "I guess this is all you need from me. I have a spare if you ever lose this or lock yourself out or something else I'm sure you won't do."

"Good to know." He took the key with a distracting smile.

I was also thinking about how I would have had to wash out my brush if he'd let me help. The silence got slightly awkward.

A gray car pulled into the remaining space to draw both our attention and relieve the silence. "There's my help," Simon said.

The front door opened and a surprisingly familiar face exited the driver's seat.

"Hey, Jackson," Simon called out. "You lost, huh?"

Jackson answered as he walked up to join us. "I won the first one. Noah insisted on two out of three. When I lost that, Dan made us do three out of five because he wanted a break from hearing about flavor-enhanced pepperoni. Yet here I am, so my Rock, Paper, Scissors skills must need some work."

A delightful sense of belonging swept over me as I recognized the names and even why one of them was tired of hearing about pepperoni.

Simon shook his head. "I'm sure Noah's latest idea is as brilliant as always."

"Hi, Cassidy," Jackson said.

"You guys have met?" Simon asked.

I nodded.

"I broke her lamp yesterday," Jackson said. "That's who you have helping you move."

"Great. Why aren't you better at Rock, Paper, Scissors?" Simon's sarcasm was playful.

Jackson shrugged apologetically.

"I'm sure Simon has better quality furniture," I said. "And you didn't break it." I was talking to Jackson, but I mostly wanted Simon to know he hadn't really broken anything.

Jackson tried to hide a smile as he squinted doubtfully at me. Then he got more serious as he turned to Simon. "Dan does want me back at four though so we better get started."

Simon nodded and both guys gave me a farewell glance.

"Have fun," I said, "and I'll be here if you have any questions." I closed the door before my face could turn red. I was already embarrassed in advance of anyone asking me a question. I'd walked through Granny's old apartment earlier to note things – like the main water valve – that Mr. Franks had shown me. I was sure I was clueless about being a landlord, and apparently about what else I could call myself.

I returned to my white wall project. It did somehow look cleaner where I had painted even though I couldn't really say the

48

rest of the wall looked dirty. Maybe customers would think it was an improvement. Someone might come in, smell fresh paint, and take that as a sign that I was keeping the place well-maintained. Someone might also come in, smell fresh paint, and only care that paint smelled bad.

I frowned at the realization that a bad smell would likely be worse for someone selling flowers than someone selling knickknacks. This would not be awesome for my relationship with Sarah, even if she had suggested I paint the whole wall. I stared at her currently empty section of the store. She had a chair and a card table for a desk. There was a cooler with glass doors and a weird round bin with water in the bottom. Neither displayed flowers at the moment. I imagined the beautiful bouquets on display during the week.

Sarah had called the police the day Granny died. She was worried when Granny wasn't there to let her in or open the shop. She didn't have the number for anyone in the family. Mom had been notified as the next of kin.

We set to work planning a funeral and left Granny's Shelf closed for several days while we figured out how to move forward. When we met with Mrs. Sweet to discuss the will, it became clear that Granny was wealthier than anyone knew. She lived simply by choice. She left a generous sum to her favorite charity and the same amount to my mom, my sister and my brother. The rest – which was a lot – went to me with the condition that I take over the care of her store and her brother.

My mom did not seem surprised that my share was more. My brother shrugged it off as necessary for the work she asked, work he did not want. But my sister was livid. Ava said nothing at first,

49

certainly not in front of the lawyer or the rest of the family. She called me the next day and demanded that I give her half my inheritance. I told her I was already thinking of dividing it more fairly, but I needed time to read the financial records. David seemed to think Granny's Shelf was operating at a loss, and I had no idea what Jojo's expenses were. I said I would eventually give some money to her and to Mom and David.

That's when Ava nearly exploded. I could still hear the echo of that nasty conversation.

"Don't you *dare* tell them I wanted more money!"

"I didn't say I would—"

"Of course you will," Ava snapped. "You always do this. You always try to make me look bad."

She'd accused me of that before, but never so fiercely. I had no response.

"You want people to think you're such a perfect little saint," she continued with venom. "You think you're everyone's favorite all the time. I changed my mind. I don't want a single cent from you. You keep all the money so everyone will know what a miserable failure your life is. You won't be able to run that business even with ridiculous funding. And I will enjoy seeing you fail. The only sad part will be when you take Uncle Jojo and that flower woman down with you."

"What flower woman?" Nothing Ava said made sense. I asked about the flower woman because it was the last confusing thing.

She laughed cruelly. "You're so wrapped up in your selfish world that you don't even know all her flowers are wilting while you keep the shop closed. Who knows how many customers she's already lost because of your incompetence." She hung up before I could even try to say anything.

But when I realized she meant Sarah Franks, I pieced together that Sarah had called the police when she couldn't get in to check on Granny. She didn't have a key. Keeping the store closed until I could run it full time was continuing to affect her flower sales. I felt horrible for being so blind.

I looked at my work schedule and figured out which hours I could be at Granny's Shelf until I'd served out my notice. Then I called Sarah and left a message with that information. I also printed a page with those hours to stick on the front door. Sarah showed up all those hours. She replaced the dead flowers without giving me a single dirty look. But we barely spoke. The tension was super uncomfortable.

While I wanted to improve my relationship with Ava, she'd explicitly told me not to call her. Time and patience was the best strategy there. Building a relationship with Sarah needed present effort. I sensed that she wanted us to get along, too, and didn't know how to do that any better than I did. At least now we could talk about paint fumes and comparing the white wall to the other white walls. That was going to be fascinating fodder for conversation. I rolled my eyes at the thought as I set my brush across the top of the paint can.

Someone had knocked on my back door. I assumed it was either Simon or Jackson, though I didn't know which I hoped to see. There was an equal chance of embarrassing myself in front of either. I checked to confirm I still had only one drip of paint on my shirt, then ran my hand down the braid on my back to smooth it *before* I checked to confirm there was no paint on my hands.

It was Simon. His cheeks were pink and his hair slightly damp from working in the sun. If anything, he looked better than before the exertion. He was holding a dusty doormat with sunflowers on it. "Do you want this?" he asked.

The mat was old and vaguely familiar. The fact that I couldn't immediately place it must have shown in my expression.

"It was at the top of the stairs," Simon explained. "Must have belonged to your grandmother and..." He lifted his eyebrows in a way that repeated his earlier question.

"Oh, yeah." I'd stepped on that mat so many times I'd stopped seeing it, somehow didn't register it wasn't attached when we cleaned out the apartment. But did I want it? "Do you want it?" I asked.

"I... don't think I need it. And I probably wouldn't have chosen flowers." He spoke slowly and ended with a wince of apology for not loving the sunflower motif.

I felt bad for putting him on the spot and reached for the mat. "Well, I don't have a mat at my place and... I guess this'll do."

"Okay. Good." He was already moving away as he said, "Take care."

It was hard to wave while holding a dirty doormat so I simply nodded before I closed the door. I set the mat near the locker in the back so I wouldn't forget to take it home. Then I washed my hands. Dirt would not disappear in the white paint. I had just dipped the brush in the can when I heard another knock.

Maybe it was Jackson this time. Maybe I could show him my I-don't-know-what-you're-talking-about face, too.

Simon was behind my door again. "Hi," he said, sheepish this time. "I meant to ask when I was just here... I'd like to put

52

some blackout curtains in the bedroom, and I don't think the rods in there will support them. Do you mind if I hang something sturdier?"

Did I mind if he did some work? "No," I said. "No, that's fine."

"Great. I didn't want to go poking holes in the place without your permission."

I caught sight of Jackson over his shoulder carrying a fairly large drum from the back of the truck. It was taller but with a smaller diameter than a bass and had what looked like little feet on one end. When he saw me looking, he tipped it to the side to pretend he was dropping it. My smile vanished as the antic caused him to really lose his grip. Fortunately, a quick lunge got it secure in his arms before it hit the ground and before Simon turned around.

"Careful with that, man."

"I got it," Jackson said. "No reason to worry I might drop it." He sounded guilty.

Simon turned back slowly, as though he wasn't sure he should take his eyes off his help. I think I was as relieved as Jackson that he'd caught it, but Simon's suspicion had brought back my amusement. I schooled my face as his eyes met mine.

"All right. If new rods are good, I'll get out of your hair. Again."

"That's still fine," I said. It *was* still fine, but I was tense enough that it felt like a weird thing to say. I closed the door on his retreating back as quickly as I could without slamming it.

Back to my project I went. I got a few feet painted before there was yet another knock. I was about to smooth my hair when I realized I forgot to put down the paintbrush. I kept the hand with the brush hidden behind the door as I opened it. I wasn't surprised that it was Simon or that I quickly felt as flushed as he looked.

"Sorry to keep bothering you," he said. "I think I'm almost done, and um… I'm not returning the truck until tomorrow because of… long story. Anyway, will it be a problem if it sits here overnight?"

I glanced at the truck long enough to notice Jackson's car was no longer parked next to it. "I don't see how it would be a problem," I said. "You can park whatever you want in your space."

"Thanks. I didn't know if it might block something or…" He held his hands out to surrender the rest of his sentence to other unknowns.

"Yeah. It was considerate of you to ask but not a problem."

"Good," he said. "I really am almost done. I'm going to leave as soon as my ride gets here so you don't have to wait around if you're waiting."

I was suddenly glad I hadn't put down the brush. I moved it in front of me as I said, "I'm still here because I'm working."

He rewarded my illustration with a dazzling smile. "I'll leave you to finish then, and I'll see you around."

"Glad you got moved in okay."

He waved, and I waved the paintbrush before I hid behind my closed door. Then I finally got the side wall completely white. I washed out my brush before I walked around the shop surveying my work. It was good. I could see the slight change in shade at the corners only because I knew it was there. Most anyone else would assume it was the lighting. A bit of peace settled over me. Painting that wall had given me a stronger sense of ownership than my name on the deed. I reflected on the events of the day and that I had successfully answered all of Simon's questions. There was a possibility that I would not be a completely terrible... person who rents an apartment to another person. I was kind of excited about coming back to flip the open sign in the morning.

6

$\mathcal{T}$he next morning, I parked next to a big truck. It still didn't present any problems. It prompted a memory of Jackson pretending to fumble his load and his expression when he lost control. Both brought a smile to my face. And then I registered the fact that he had been carrying a drum. I guessed I'd rented the space right above me to someone who played the drums.

Mrs. Sweet told me that Simon was a songwriter. I hadn't made the connection that the job could involve playing instruments. Or drums. I shrugged that off as something to worry about when and if it became something to worry about. The present had enough worries.

Sarah was coming. I heard the wheels of her cart of flowers crossing the street behind me. The greenhouse was essentially next door, just that narrow street between. She'd probably been watching for me to arrive. Her hair was shorter than mine, only a bit past her shoulders, and a darker brown. She seemed to put more effort into making hers look nice. Today she had a French braid that wrapped around the back of her head and over her shoulder. The last time I saw her, there had been a small braid holding the front back. I wished I could be more creative than the same high braid I did whenever I did anything.

"Good morning," I called, trying to look as though I wasn't faking a smile. I wasn't faking it, but the thought that she might think I was made me too self-conscious to feel natural.

"Hi, Cassidy," she said. She pointed at the truck she was passing. "Simon is moving in?"

"He unloaded it yesterday and said he was going to return the truck this morning."

She nodded.

"I'll get the door." I hurried to get the key in the lock and then held it open for her cart to pass through.

"Thanks." She smiled at me, then went to the front to start organizing a pretty display.

I sat at my desk and opened a ledger. I had resolved that this was the day I'd stop thinking of Granny's financial records as off-limits. They were mine now, and I wasn't snooping. I was operating a business. Plus, with real work in front of me, I wasn't just sitting there ignoring Sarah.

I became shockingly engrossed in the records. I did well in math, but it was never my favorite subject. The numbers on Granny's pages and screens weren't just numbers. Each one represented the work of a local artisan, an item hand-picked for a new home, or even something Granny designed herself. These numbers were Granny's means of keeping a roof over her head and providing enough to be generous to others. I was inspired by her records and found new joy in serving the customers who interrupted me.

I wasn't unrealistic. I knew a lot of the trinkets I sold would collect dust until they were thrown away or end up forgotten in the bottom of a suitcase. But I left room for hope that some would be keepsakes of favorite vacations or mementos of kids who had grown up and moved out. And some would just be really pretty decorations. Life needed beauty.

By Thursday, my studying phase was over. I'd still need to check those records regularly and keep them updated. I knew where to find everything though. I felt confident, confident enough to start a conversation that would be more than two sentences. I left my desk even though there were no customers. I walked right up to Sarah's corner and leaned over to smell the closest bouquet.

I said, "You've been busy today." A couple had come in to talk about flowers for their wedding. I understood that Sarah had not done many weddings so it was a big deal.

"Yeah," she said. "I love it when people don't already know exactly what they want and let me make suggestions."

"All of these arrangements look great." I gestured towards her cooler. "I think people would be wise to listen to your suggestions."

"Thank you." Her gratitude was sincere, but her eyes dropped quickly.

I hoped she was thinking of something to say because I was already out of ideas.

"What did Simon want?" she asked.

"Simon?"

"Wasn't Simon Donnelly in here this morning? I hope there isn't a problem upstairs."

"Oh, right. No." He'd been there between customers several hours ago so I'd sort of forgotten. "I mean, there wasn't a problem. He said he found a pan in the back of a cupboard, something that I guess we missed. You know, now that I think about it, it's weird that he didn't just give me the pan. He came in to tell me that he was going to give me the pan."

"Huh." Sarah appeared to consider that. "Maybe he didn't want to give it to you in front of customers?" She didn't sound convinced that was a good reason.

"Maybe?" I said. "Or maybe he forgot and didn't want to go back for it right then."

Sarah shrugged. Then she grinned. "He's cute, isn't he?"

"That's an understatement."

We both laughed. We sobered quickly as someone came in to buy one of the bouquets.

I stepped out of the way but stayed nearby. We probably couldn't speculate on the absent pan much longer, but I didn't want to give up the momentum.

Jackson came in before the man finished paying. "Hi, Cassidy." He must have noticed I was surprised to see him because he explained right away. "I'm here to talk to Sarah, but I need to wait my turn."

"Feel free to look around while you wait." I motioned to a shelf.

"Staying in professional mode?"

"What? You're *not* here to buy a new music box?" I grabbed a carousel and began to wind it.

"How did you know I collected music boxes, and…" Jackson dropped the joke when he failed to keep a straight face. "What do *you* think of that?"

"This?" I flipped it on. I didn't recognize the melody after a few tinkly notes and turned it back off. "I'm not really a music box person, but I like that it turns while it plays. That's kind of cool."

He seemed to agree with my assessment before he pointed to the shelf. "Which of these items would you be most likely to take home?"

I returned the music box as I answered. "The Mary statue."

"That was a fast answer," he said. "Have you been thinking about keeping that one?"

"No, I… I don't collect anything really. I just like to admire religious art. I like statues and candles and… pretty chalices… and stained glass is awesome."

"Hey, Jackson." The door was closing on Sarah's last customer. "What does your mom want this week?"

His mom? There was my chance to ask while it was relevant. "Who is your mom?"

He chuckled at my question as though I was kidding before he turned to Sarah. "She said pink. Then she told me she was wanting something extra girly this week so I'm going to let you decide what that means."

Sarah quickly turned to study her flowers.

Jackson glanced back and did a double take. "Oh, were you serious? You really don't know who my mom is?"

"How is that surprising?" I asked. "I just met you, and you didn't tell me."

He still seemed a little confused. That tipped my guess towards Mrs. Donnelly since he'd been there with Simon. I couldn't put my finger on why I thought they'd acted more like friends than brothers, but it kept me from making the guess out loud. Then a slow smile appeared on his face. "You know, it isn't often a guy gets an air of mystery in a small town. I don't think I'm going to tell you."

"You think refusing to answer a simple question gives you an air of mystery?"

There was a hint of hesitation before he answered. "Yes. I'm sticking with air of mystery. I like the sound of that."

Sarah had opened up three bouquets on her table and was redistributing the contents. I could tell she was listening though because she was trying not to laugh.

"Will you tell me who his mom is?"

Jackson gasped.

Sarah laughed. "I think air of ridiculous is more like it, but I won't interfere."

"I told Cassidy she should join us at St. Jude's tomorrow night," Jackson said. "Have you been helping me convince her?"

"I didn't know I was supposed to be convincing her." Sarah's eyes flicked towards me with a hint of apology, likely more because we'd barely talked at all than because we hadn't talked about that specific topic. "But it is a good group if you want to come."

Jackson would not be the only familiar face I'd see. "How many people come each week? Usually?" I glanced between the two of them as I asked.

Jackson looked at Sarah for the answer.

"Jackson's actually kind of new himself," she said.

He shrugged. "It would have been pretty hard to drive up from West Virginia every week."

"I suppose school is a good excuse," Sarah said. "Anyway, I think there's probably eight or ten people you can count on being there every week with enough people who come occasionally to make it at least fifteen most weeks. We split up to have two smaller groups when it feels crowded." She'd been wrapping up flowers as she spoke. "I think this says extra girly."

I saw several shades of pink and a couple of white carnations – one of the few flowers I could name – as she handed it to Jackson.

"I will take your word for that." He passed her a credit card and wished us both a nice day as he took it back and left with the bouquet. It was for his mom. I knew a part of me was happy to know it wasn't for a girlfriend. But when he came in, he didn't say he was there to get flowers for his mom. He'd said he was there to talk to Sarah. Was he picking up his mom's flowers to be a good son or because he was interested in Sarah? I cared about that mystery more than the identity of his mom.

Jackson left a loud silence when he left the store. Tension seeped back into the space between me and Sarah. I told her I should check some order dates and went back to my desk to open Granny's book of supplier notes.

I had jumped through a lot of hoops to get all her accounts switched to my name. Most of it wasn't actually difficult. But I knew that for a while, every time I picked up that book I was going to remember the poor guy who had tripped all over himself trying to be super sensitive to the situation.

Though we both saw a few more customers, the rest of the afternoon was fairly quiet. I could not say the same thing about Friday morning. It began normal enough. Sarah arrived right after me. We managed a bit of small talk about how we'd likely be busier heading into the weekend. Then she organized her already neat display while I skimmed through familiar records.

Something began to thump on the ceiling. It didn't sound like a drum. It sounded more like a person stomping or jumping. Then there were alternating high and low notes on a piano or keyboard. The tone changed to settle my guess on keyboard. The notes were interspersed in a regular pattern. But the wide range still made it more noise than melody. And the thumping came back. It wasn't annoying, somehow, just curious.

I glanced at Sarah. She glanced back. The stomping suddenly got louder, and we cracked up at the same time.

"What is he doing?" she asked.

"I have no idea."

She giggled a bit as she caught her breath. "I don't think that's the next hymn to be published."

I shook my head. "Maybe it's, like, part of the process."

"The process?"

"I don't know," I said. "Don't creative types have... rituals for getting the creative juices going or something like that?"

Sarah tipped her head thoughtfully.

It hit me that she was an artist. Her flower arrangements were beautiful proof of that. "Do you?" I asked. "Do you have some kind of system or... Do you ever not know how to arrange the flowers?"

"Yeah. Sometimes I don't like what I put together and have to really think about how to make it better," she said. "I usually just start over. I don't think there's anything I would call a process or..." During her search for words, whatever was happening upstairs seemed to finish with a burst of successive low notes. She pointed at the ceiling. "I don't think that would help."

We both laughed again but quit as a pair of older women came in to get some flowers. Sarah had to run to the greenhouse to find enough of the kind one wanted. I knew she literally ran as soon as she was outside so they would not be waiting long. They both knew my grandmother and talked to me briefly about how they hoped I enjoyed taking over and would pray for my success. They were sweet, though they made me feel super young, almost as though they might have used the same tone to wish me luck on my first day of kindergarten. Sarah sent them home delighted with their flowers.

It was only a few minutes later when Simon came in carrying a shallow tub. He nodded a greeting at Sarah as he passed, then walked up holding the tub out to me with a smile that made me feel warm all over. "Here you go, Cassidy."

"What's this?" I asked, apparently feeling warm *and* stupid.

"I told you I'd return the pan I found in the back of the cupboard."

"Oh, right. I... uh... when you said pan, I was thinking something for cooking and..." I fought the fog for some way to finish the sentence I'd unnecessarily ended with and.

Simon saved me with a gracious expression. "It has been a few days since I mentioned it so I can see why you'd forget."

"I wonder if I can think of a use for this." I focused on the plastic pan. That was easier than the handsome face.

"Looks like it'd be good for catching leaks," he said.

"Hmm. I might have to hope I don't find a use for it then."

"Maybe you can find someone to give it to, but... uh..." He waved off his own suggestion as he seemed to realize it might sound like wishing leaks on someone else. "Well, I gotta run anyway. Have a nice weekend."

"Thanks," I said, holding up the pan. I stuffed it in my locker and turned back to see Simon wave through the big front window.

"Do you think he knows we could hear him?" Sarah said.

I thought we might share another laugh, but the moment had passed. We just looked at each other awkwardly before retreating into separate tasks. Fortunately, there were not a ton of awkward moments as at least one customer was in the shop most of the day.

I was dusting off some shelves during a quiet stretch shortly before closing time when Jojo entered. He walked straight past me before I could say anything. I followed him to my desk where he slapped down a yellow sticky note. There was a smiley face drawn on it.

"Oh, thank you," I said.

He dipped into his customary bow, then sent another in Sarah's direction.

"Hi, Jojo," she called.

He walked over to the wall that used to have a door. He rubbed one hand against it, then turned to me with an exaggerated shrug.

"We moved the door to the outside to rent the apartment to Simon Donnelly," I said. "Did you see the new door outside?" I pointed to where it was on the other side of the wall.

Jojo tapped his palm against the wall again. His eyes came back to mine with a plea for information. Mom hadn't found anything she thought might belong to him and guessed he just needed time to get used to the change.

"It does look different in here without the door," I said.

Jojo turned around and put both hands on the wall about shoulder height. It was covered so well I couldn't be sure, but I thought his hands might be resting where either side of the frame had been. I didn't know what else to say about the missing door. He'd been in the store long enough for me to notice that he did not smell good. One issue with his self-care was not bathing often enough. I didn't really want to say something, but it was my job now. Granny had always been matter-of-fact with him about it.

"I think it's time for you to take a shower, Uncle Jojo."

He turned to face me with one hand palm up. He put the other hand on top and rubbed it in a circle.

I knew he made that sign often when talking about food. "Do you want to get something to eat first?" I guessed.

He didn't answer me but immediately moved towards the front door. I took that to mean he was on his way to get dinner, and then a shower.

Sarah waved as he passed her.

Jojo stopped two steps from the exit. He turned back and pointed to one of the bouquets in her bin.

"Which flower do you like?" she asked.

He pointed again.

"Yellow?"

When he nodded, she pulled out the bouquet to open it and gave him a yellow flower.

Jojo left smiling. I approached as Sarah unwrapped the rest of the bunch.

"Thanks for giving him a flower," I said. "My grandmother's journal said you've given him a few and didn't charge her. Uh… you don't have to keep the same deal you had with her. If you want me to keep a tally of…"

Sarah shooed away my offer before I finished it. "No. It's really nothing. He's always happy to take just one."

"You're sure?"

She nodded and seemed sincere.

"Okay. Well, it's Friday so I guess I'll see you at St. Jude's after dinner. Right?"

"Yeah. I'll be there."

I flipped the sign to closed and locked the door. We both needed a few minutes to gather our things. We did so in total silence since I'd already mentioned seeing her later, which felt like parting words.

There was a school behind the church. The notice in the bulletin had given a room number. I opened one of the glass doors and immediately heard voices down a hallway to my left. I figured the room I was looking for would be that way.

Around the corner, I saw two women who appeared to be around my mom's age standing inside a large plastic fence with several toddlers. One of the women had a baby strapped to her front. The picture was missing anyone from my generation. The woman with the baby smiled brightly and called out to me. "Are you looking for the young adult group?"

"I am."

She waved me towards her. "Keep coming. It's right up here on your left."

By the time I got to the door she indicated, a woman had come from inside to meet me. This woman also had a baby in her arms, but she didn't look a lot older than me. "Hi, I'm Emily," she said.

"I'm Cassidy."

"Welcome," Emily said. "Come on in." She ushered me into a room where three couples were sitting with a guy I assumed was with Emily.

I felt conspicuously alone and had to fight an impulse to turn around.

Emily took the seat next to that extra guy and patted the chair on her other side for me. "This is Cassidy, everyone. We'll need nametags today."

"I'm on it." One of the other women was fishing in a bag next to her chair. She pulled out a marker and a sheet of white stickers.

Emily began to quiz me while the others passed around nametags.

"Are you new to Andauk or to St. Jude's or..." She waved her hand to get me to fill in the right answer.

"Well, I actually went to church here when I was little, but we moved when I was ten," I explained. "I just moved back."

"Ah. You're the one who took over Granny's Shelf for Mrs. Johnson?"

"Yeah."

"Cool. My husband and I run a place down the street if you need anything, Joseph's Gym." She nodded at the guy next to her. "This is Joseph."

I smiled to acknowledge the introduction.

He pointed at the label he'd just slapped on to confirm it.

"How did you hear about our group?" Emily asked.

"Mostly the bulletin."

"Mostly?"

69

"A guy named Jackson also told me about it." I briefly thought about asking his last name. But I didn't want to give the impression of too much interest.

Emily accepted it as a casual mention. "Oh, you know what? You are actually living in my old apartment."

"I am?" The woman I just met knew where I worked and where I lived. Small towns were kind of scary. Jackson might have been slightly justified to laugh when I didn't know who his mom was.

"Someone else lived there between us so don't blame me for," Emily shrugged with a laugh, "well, anything there might be to blame someone for."

I smiled at her light tone. It also helped me relax that I'd seen three other women enter, including Sarah, and they all entered alone, too. I made a mental note to get there five minutes later next week.

"Anyway, Mr. Franks is great." Emily flashed a smile at Sarah as she said it. "If you have to call him because something is broken, he'll totally come over and make you feel like you're doing him a favor by putting him to work."

"I'll try to remember that if I do have a problem."

"It'll probably be fine for you though," Emily said. "I think most of my problems were my fault. How old are you? I heard you were practically still a kid, but you look like an adult to me."

"I'm twenty-three."

"Young but not still a kid," Emily said. "That makes sense."

Jackson came in with that Noah guy from Pans and Plates.

They remained standing next to a few other people who came in after the seats were full. They both smiled in recognition when they saw me. I gave a quick wave of greeting.

"Okay, everyone, it's already after seven." One of the guys from the other couples – his nametag said Gabriel – picked up a notebook as he looked around the room. Gabriel seemed to be in charge so I turned towards him and not deliberately away from Jackson.

"Full group today," Gabriel said. "We'll begin with a prayer together, then split up."

Several heads nodded as they all bowed.

Gabriel asked God to bless our time together with fruitful discussion, that at least one person would hear something he or she needed to hear, and that we'd remember to honor him in all we did. His words sounded practiced but genuine. We all joined in for an Our Father. Then Gabriel got up and said, "Let's go, guys."

I think I would have figured out pretty quickly that we were separating along gender lines even if Emily hadn't explained that the guys were moving to the classroom next door. A few of the women rearranged to make our new circle smaller. Sarah ended up next to me. Attention shifted to the redhead next to Gabriel's vacated chair. She was also the woman who had passed out nametags and written Ruth on hers.

"Let's start with some personal business," she said. "I know we all want to ask Ella how she's feeling with only two weeks to go so we'll do it as a group."

I found the right nametag as the others turned to her.

Ella had low pigtails and a very round belly, which she ran her hand over as she spoke. "I guess the good news is that the more

71

uncomfortable I get, the less scared I get. I think I'm ready to find out what labor feels like."

"That's good," Emily said, "because you're going to find out."

Ruth said, "And Sebastian is still doting on you properly?"

Ella didn't seem to know how to answer. Her face began to turn red.

"Time to move on to Heather." Ruth directed her gaze and mine to the woman on her other side. "You have *three* weeks before your big day. No hiccups in the wedding planning?"

"No. It's going to be awesome."

"Wonderful. *I'm* looking forward to it." Ruth looked at me next. "Cassidy is new this week. Did everyone say hi to Cassidy?"

There was a chorus of greetings that made me feel as though I was back in elementary school. I believe Ruth intended that because we were technically in an elementary school, what I thought might be the music room. I wasn't the only one who smiled at the nostalgia of the moment.

"So Cassidy," Ruth said. "What brings you here? What do you hope to get from this group?"

I wanted to say something wise like spiritual growth. But I was brave enough to tell the whole truth. "Well, my faith is the most important thing to me so I thought going somewhere people shared it might be a good place to find some friends."

The nodding around me suggested I'd given a fine answer. Maybe that was a sign it was true. I'd never been good at making friends. When I was little, I mostly hung out with Ava and her friends. They graduated three years ahead of me. High school was lonely after that. My relationship with God had blossomed during that time though so I wasn't sad when I remembered. I joined the campus ministry when I started college and found two girls I got along with well. I dropped out of school after my first year though, and we had only been in touch online since.

"Are you dating anyone?"

I heard the question before I realized Ruth was still talking to me. "Oh, uh... no."

"That's important," Ruth said, "because some of us like to look for matchmaking possibilities."

"Plus, one of the guys might ask about you," Emily added.

"Oh, she's super cute. They're all going to ask."

I couldn't read her sloppy handwriting, though her name started with a J. Her comment must have made me blush because Ruth said they'd embarrassed enough people, and it was time to begin the discussion.

"Gabriel and I picked St. Philip Neri for inspiration this week," Ruth continued. "His nickname is 'the laughing saint.' I know we've touched on this before, but we wanted to start with some reflection on the difference between joy as a fruit of the Holy Spirit and just regular happiness."

"Happiness is fleeting," someone said.

"Yeah. Joy is lasting."

"It's also deeper," Emily said. "I mean, it can be there even on top of other emotions. Like I remember about a year ago, one of my little ones had croup pretty bad. I mean, I wasn't worried about it being life-threatening or anything. But he couldn't sleep, and I spent a good part of the night sitting up with him and rocking him and trying to keep him calm enough that he wouldn't start wheezing. Missing out on sleep with a cranky toddler... I would not describe that as a happy time at all. But I knew I was providing comfort and love to my child. I still experienced joy from that."

"That's a great example. I agree that joy is too complex to really be called a feeling. It's more like an experience or... a gift."

"I think I also heard somewhere that joy is always... or God is always the source of joy," Heather said, "whereas happiness can come from anything. Like ice cream or chocolate."

"Though some people would argue that God is the source of everything – at least indirectly – so he is the source of happiness, too."

"I think indirectly is the key word there."

"Yeah, if you trace everyone's good choices to God, you might start attributing bad choices to God just because he made those people. But evil never comes from God."

"Inventing ice cream was a good choice."

I agreed with that, along with everyone else. I didn't contribute much but enjoyed listening to the conversation. It spiraled into a lengthy tangent at that point about favorite ice cream flavors and how none of the women who'd been pregnant had ever wanted pickles with theirs because that was a ridiculous stereotype with no basis in fact. There was also a brief discussion of which buttons on a TV remote were most useless – I lost the thread of how that connected to ice cream – before Ruth got us on track with more faith-based questions.

I was one of the last people out of the room as everyone wanted to tell me how glad they were that I came on their way out. Sarah left with me, which I recognized as a nice effort. The hallway was still crowded. The kids were being reclaimed while the two older women picked up the toys and one of the guys folded up the big fence.

Jackson and Noah were standing off to the side, and I got the impression they'd been waiting for me and Sarah, or at least one of us.

Noah waved, and Jackson said, "Hi, Sarah. Hi, Cassidy. What did you think?"

His question was directed at me, but Ruth was nearby and jumped in before I could answer.

"Oh, have you already met Ella's brother?" she asked.

I didn't answer that question either. Jackson said, "Yeah, she knows me as the guy who broke her lamp."

"You didn't break it," I said.

Ruth laughed and so did Noah. I didn't think they believed me. But if Jackson wanted people to think he broke my lamp, I wasn't going to work any harder to correct him.

"I'm going to need to hear that story later," Ruth said. She followed Gabriel towards the door.

Noah made a sweeping motion to suggest we walk that way as well.

Jackson said, "So what did you think of your first meeting, Cassidy?"

"It was great," I said. "You were right that everyone is very nice. And these ladies are smart, too."

"Of course I was right." Jackson gave a teasing smile. "And you should know that there were all kinds of really superb insights flying around in the guys' room, too. Right, Noah?"

Noah nodded with enough exaggeration to make me doubt he was thinking about anything particularly insightful. But I didn't volunteer how much time the ladies had spent talking about ice cream.

"It's still kind of weird to be back here." Jackson looked around as he spoke. "I went to school here, and I swear it was a lot bigger when I was in fifth grade."

"I know what you mean," Noah said.

"Hey! You guys are about the same age." Sarah pointed between me and Jackson. "Did you know each other when Cassidy lived here as a kid?"

Jackson eyed me thoughtfully.

"I went to public school," I said, "so probably not." We did, apparently, go to the same church, and it wasn't a huge congregation. It was somewhat likely that we'd sat in nearby pews at some point. I didn't have many memories of people around me from that time. Jackson didn't appear to come up with any either.

He got to the exit first and held the door open for the rest of us. "You are definitely coming back next week, right?"

I nodded eagerly.

"Glad we didn't scare you off."

"And you'll be back to Pans and Plates, too," Noah said. "I didn't scare you away by offering a bite of pizza?"

"No," I said.

"My dad went on and on about that after you left." Noah adopted what was clearly supposed to be his dad's tone. "What were you thinking? What kind of impression do you think that made?"

We all chuckled before Jackson looked at me shrewdly and said, "What kind of impression *did* it make?"

I played along and tried to appear more nervous than I was, though I did choose my words carefully. "Uh... well... I guess I got the impression that Noah is... passionate about his pizza."

"Nothing wrong with that," Noah said.

"I don't know." Jackson winced. "She said it like it's kind of weird."

"No, I didn't."

"You kind of did," Sarah said.

Jackson continued to offer Noah a sympathetic expression. Noah enjoyed the teasing so I just laughed with everyone else.

Then Noah appeared to have an idea. "Oh, I'm just realizing that I don't remember the last time Sarah came in for pizza. Is this why? Because you think I'm weird?"

She didn't immediately deny it, which made Jackson laugh harder and give Noah a playful shove.

"I am so underappreciated," Noah said. He held up his hand in a wave as he began to walk away. "You all have a good night."

"See ya, man." Jackson waved and pointed to a bike against the wall with the same motion. "I know that's Sarah's ride. Where did you park, Cassidy?"

"Down that way a bit."

"I'll walk with you."

We both said goodnight to Sarah as we began to move down the sidewalk between the building and the parking lot. We only needed to pass six or seven spaces to get to my car. That suddenly felt like the most awkward length anyone could walk. It was too long to stay silent and too short to dive into a real conversation. My mind went completely blank when I coaxed it to come up with something very clever that fit in the space in front of us.

Jackson said, very casually, as though he wasn't even thinking about how much time we did or didn't have to talk, "How's Jojo?"

"He gave me a sticky note."

"He what?" Jackson sounded more curious than confused.

I didn't know why I hadn't just said Jojo was fine. Now I had to stop in front of my car to explain my random comment. "Well, I went to his place to tidy up a bit, check the mail and such. He wasn't there, and it felt wrong to go in and out of his place without... somehow acknowledging that I'd been there." I paused to see if he understood what I meant.

"That makes sense," he said. "Though your work would have been evident."

"Yeah. Anyway, I left a sticky note that said hi and had a little smiley face. The next time he came to see me, he brought a sticky note with a smiley and left it on my desk. Sometimes I get frustrated when I can't tell if I'm communicating with him or not. And this time I knew that he saw my note and liked it enough to respond. It's such a little, little thing. But it made me feel good."

"I see why it made you feel good, and I'm happy for you."

"Thanks." I pulled my keys out to fiddle with as I felt uncertain as to why I thanked him. He said something nice to hear. I guessed gratitude was appropriate.

"Well, I'm walking home so I'll continue from here and let you go. Goodnight."

I nodded with a quick wave and scurried to my car. I tried not to watch him walking, afraid he might catch me watching and also afraid of confirming that he wasn't going to look back anyway.

I spent some time reflecting on the day after I got home, the good parts and the not-so-good parts. I made a list of things I wanted to talk to God about. I replayed a few conversations. A clue jumped out at me that I'd missed at the time. Ruth said that Jackson was Ella's brother. Ella was expecting a baby very soon, and Mrs. Sweet had talked more than once about how excited she was to be on the verge of becoming a grandmother. Jackson's last name might be Sweet. Now I had something to talk to him about. That was why I was hoping to see him again soon.

8

My heart leapt when I first saw the stack. Jojo wasn't home again. I moved to sort the mail and a foot-high stack of sticky notes sat on the table next to it. The whole stack was lined up perfectly with the corner of the table. It appeared my uncle was prepared to continue the swap for some time. I did my chores first. I started some laundry, checked his fridge for anything expired, and washed a few dishes as I found one from the pizza place. I made notes on everything just like Granny did.

My fingers trembled as I reached out to peel off the top sticky note. That was evidence I was thinking too hard about messing up the super neat stack. I reminded myself it was something I could fix, then peeled off a note with no trouble. I drew a flower instead of a smiley and wrote I love you under it.

When I opened the door to leave, a gray cat zipped inside and made a beeline for the food dish in the corner. The dish was empty. The cat stared at it. I stared at the cat. I didn't know if either of us knew what all the staring was supposed to accomplish. Eventually, I walked over and stared at the cat from much closer.

It looked up and meowed at me.

"Hello, kitty," I said. "Where did you come from?"

I got the response I expected, which was nothing. I squatted down to see if it would let me pet it. The cat leaned into my hand and closed its eyes. I could see why Jojo liked it.

"Since I have no idea when Jojo might be back to feed you or let you out again, you should probably leave with me." I was thinking out loud more than talking to the animal. I didn't have much experience with cats, but I managed to pick it up without hurting it or having my face clawed. I set it down again once I had the door closed behind us. The cat walked around my ankles, then dashed off into some nearby bushes.

I went home and called my mom. I told her about the cat and that things seemed to be going okay for me in general. She asked if I'd seen "that Jackson kid" again. I said he was at the church meeting on Friday without letting on that we'd talked one-on-one at all. There was no point raising her hopes or mine that we were becoming friends.

She asked if I'd made a decision about calling my dad. She moved on as soon as I said no because she'd already made it clear she wouldn't interfere in my decision when I'd asked for advice.

I had only vague memories of my dad, which meant I really didn't know him. I couldn't figure out how I was supposed to know if I wanted to know someone I didn't know. And I didn't know why it only seemed complicated to *me*. Ava had been excited to have a chance to talk to Dad. David was adamant that the man had given up any right to a relationship with his children. They'd made opposite choices, yet they'd both made it seem those choices were easy. I did not understand.

\*\*\*\*

81

Every day I thought the paint smell had dissipated until I walked in the next morning and smelled it again. I spent some time looking for sparse areas to restock. There were more on the back shelves, but I kept walking back to the front because I was trying to decide if the paint smell was stronger near the front or the back of the store. I made a few trips even after I finished my stocking, which felt like a sign I was on the verge of becoming bored. Sarah might have thought I was pacing. I didn't want to explain that I was smelling the air.

Perhaps I could start a related conversation without admitting my study of fumes. She was reading a book. I tried to watch for signs she didn't want to be interrupted, but she set it aside when she noticed my approach.

"How long do you think it will take the paint smell to go away completely?" I asked.

Her shoulders lifted with a huge inhale. "I... don't really smell it anymore."

"Not even when you first come in?"

"No. I don't think so." She sounded apologetic. "Maybe because I usually come in surrounded by flowers."

"Good point," I said. And maybe the flowers up front meant it wasn't my imagination that the paint was stronger by the back door. "Those are different, the jars. I don't think I've seen you put flowers in jars before."

"I haven't. But I think they came out pretty well." Behind Sarah, on her cart, were eight mason jars filled with colorful stones with ribbons and flowers spraying out the top. She turned one slowly to view all sides while she talked about it. "They're centerpieces for some sort of corporate event. I was nervous when

I quoted a price because I had to buy all this extra stuff she wanted, but she seemed to think it was reasonable. She liked the picture I sent, too, so as long as she doesn't have a different opinion when she sees them in person... well, I might just add a picture to the options on my website."

I nodded.

"Oh, is he coming in?" Sarah's voice was furtive.

I looked up to see Simon outside the window, and he did in fact reach for the door to enter.

"Hey, Sarah. Cassidy."

"Hi, Simon. Do you need something?" I looked towards Sarah because it seemed more likely he'd buy flowers than anything I was selling.

Sarah also greeted him and looked at me as though I was more likely to have an answer.

"Not exactly," Simon said. He focused on me. "I'm expecting a package later today, and it occurred to me that it's not really obvious from the front that there's a B address on the side, and I thought it might get delivered here. I just wanted to say that if someone brings you a package for me, you can just put it aside and text me to come get it. You don't have to try to bring it to me or anything."

"Oh. Okay. That should be fine."

"Are you sure?" Simon asked. "I mean, if you tell the guy he needs to leave it over by the side door, he'd probably do that."

"It's probably more secure to leave whatever it is in here than in that narrow walkway," I said, "though I don't think theft is much of a problem in Andauk."

"No, it's not.  But I don't want to put you out."  He eyed me with concern over the hardship he was causing.

The expression made me desperate to lighten the moment. "This isn't a package that needs a forklift to move, right?  I'm sure I can set it aside without feeling burdened."

"It's not that big," he said, still serious.  "Thank you for taking care of it.  Hope you both have a nice day."

I wished him the same and so did Sarah.  We watched him walk out and past the window again.  When I couldn't think of anything to say other than pointing out again what a nice-looking man he was, I went to my desk to look for something I could organize.

The stomping began a minute later.  It was loud enough that I thought he must be landing with both feet.  But the rhythm seemed too controlled.  I could only picture stomping.  When the high and low notes joined in, I glanced at Sarah.

She lifted her eyes to the ceiling and back with confusion.  It didn't seem quite as funny to either of us as it had the first time.  I knew it was because that undercurrent of tension had returned.  It was worse than the paint fumes at returning unexpectedly.  In that moment, I also had the clarity to know it would keep coming back until I apologized.

I didn't take the most direct route to Sarah.  My nerves insisted that I straighten a few shelves here and there.  But when I did get close, I took a deep breath and got directly to the point. "Sarah, I'm sorry," I said.  "I'm sorry that you got locked out so long after Granny died.  I didn't even think about how it would affect you or your business, and that was selfish of me."

84

"Oh." She seemed temporarily speechless. We simply stared at each other, more uncomfortable than ever.

I started to think I needed to walk away and give her time to forgive me.

But then she started to shake her head. "It's not... Your grandmother died. I never thought it was selfish to need some time to process that. I was actually... I didn't know if anyone would ever reopen the store – or let me stay if they did. I felt awful for wondering about how the death of a really nice woman might affect me financially."

"But it did affect you," I said. "A lot of flowers wilted before you could sell them."

She shrugged. "I lost some flowers, but not a lot."

"Did you lose customers, too?"

"Maybe a few walk-ins, but all the regulars just came to the house. Fortunately, no one complained."

"Did someone complain before?"

"Oh, yeah. That's how I ended up here." Sarah waved her hands to visually carve out her corner of the store.

I realized there was backstory that could be relevant for me as her not-landlord to know. "Granny just told me you were going to start selling flowers here," I said. "She didn't give details. How *did* you end up here?"

"Uh... well, maybe I should start at the beginning."

"Yes."

"It's my mom's greenhouse, at least originally. My dad built it for her shortly after they got married. I started helping her – and learning from her – when I was still very young. It was always just a hobby for her. But when I was in high school, I started to see the potential for selling the flowers. St. Jude's was my first customer. I convinced someone in the office there that we could provide a beautiful bouquet for the altar each week. I made a bunch of corsages for prom my senior year. Then I got a case, that one actually," she pointed to the cooler behind her, "in the grocery store.

"That was a big investment and... wait... before I talked my parents into investing in the cooler, I created a website. My brother helped me with that. And we got a few orders and put an advertisement for the site on top of the cooler. The grocery store took a cut of what sold out of the cooler, but we started to get quite a bit of traffic on the site where people could enter more custom orders. As more people started coming by the house to pick up their flowers, some of the neighbors complained about the traffic and people parking in the grass and..." She sounded remorseful about the inconvenience. "I was so excited about being able to earn income from something I loved, and I didn't fully consider how it might affect others. One guy had to come over and ask which of our customers was blocking his driveway."

I nodded at her to keep going with the story. I felt sympathy for the neighbors and for Sarah.

"My mom and I – she's still my business partner – were thinking we might have to start accepting orders for delivery only. That would mean fewer parked cars, but we'd be going in and out all the time and... honestly, we set our delivery fee high to deliberately discourage deliveries and it mostly works. We never wanted to spend more time driving than arranging flowers. It was a lot to think and pray about. And then one of the neighbors filed an official complaint with the town council."

86

"That sounds bad," I said.

"Yeah. We got a notice that it'd be brought up at the next meeting. We apparently aren't zoned for commercial purposes, and we thought we'd be facing fines and having to shut down until we could find a suitable location to operate out of." Sarah seemed to be trying to remember the exact words of the letter, then her eyes came back to me as she relaxed.

"Fortunately, we never had to find out how bad it would be," she continued. "I was sure we were going to be forced out of business one way or another, but Evelyn invited me to bring all the flowers through her place so customers could park on Main Street to pick them up. She said she'd enjoy the company and extra foot traffic could only be good for Granny's Shelf. She made it sound like a win for everyone.

"I thought that was a really nice offer but that we'd still be in violation of something. I mean, we're still growing the flowers and using the website and having supplies delivered to our house. We're still essentially running the business from there even if people are doing the actual pickups a few yards away." She paused to smile. "Okay, it's probably more than a *few.*"

We turned to the back door together. It was more than a few yards away, and she had to go at least as far again to cross the street behind it. But I understood her point that the distance might be meaningless where a law was concerned. "Did you have to go in front of the council to argue about how this would improve the situation or something?"

"No. It was amazing. I was really glad to live in a small town where word travels fast. It seems that whoever was upset about the extra cars on the street found out we were going to shift the parking to Main Street and formally withdrew the complaint before the meeting. That meant the council took us off the agenda. Mrs. Sweet explained to me that the ordinance basically says we are free to operate a business out of our house as long as no one has a valid complaint. So your grandma's solution was perfect."

"And all this happened just a few months ago?"

Sarah nodded and said, "February."

"Wow. I can see how you'd be super stressed about trying to find a new solution when you just got this one worked out."

"I appreciate that. I still wish I could say I was upset by Evelyn's death *only* because she was a sweet lady."

I smiled because I recognized some familiarity in her words. "Yeah. I wish emotions could be less complicated, too," I said. "When I found out she left this place to me, I was kind of mad at her. I was like, why can't I just grieve for my grandmother in peace and not have to deal with the overwhelming task of trying to figure out if I'm capable of running her business?"

"Have you figured it out?" Sarah asked. "You seem pretty capable to me."

"Granny wrote everything down, which is the only reason I have any idea what I'm doing. She's teaching me even though she's not here. And while we're talking, I've learned that your rent should stay the same pretty indefinitely."

"Thanks." Sarah tipped her head thoughtfully. It looked as though she had a question, but a customer came in so we postponed the discussion until after I sold a fancy pair of salt and pepper shakers. I returned to the front thinking I had a few more questions. Sarah asked one first.

"You made it sound like your grandma didn't talk to you about taking over before she died," she said. "Were you really surprised?"

"Yes. I think I had some vague idea that the whole family would keep the store going if I thought about it at all, even though I don't know how that would have worked. And now I'm pretty sure that would *not* have worked."

Sarah smiled at my inflection as though she understood the issues of working with family. She did work with some of hers, but it seemed smooth from the outside.

"I thought about asking Granny a few times if she had plans for the store, but it seemed… insensitive somehow, that asking what might happen to her store implied she was getting old. I mean, she was almost eighty, a lot of people would have already retired. Yet I still assumed she'd live another ten years at least."

That vulnerable thought was still sitting in front of me when I noticed Jackson through the window. Sarah just gave a quick nod that she'd heard me as she also noticed and assumed he was about to come in. He greeted her first. I took that as a sign he had more interest in her if he had interest in anyone. He'd known Sarah longer so it made sense.

When he said hi to me, I said, "Hello, Jackson Sweet."

It only took a second for him to remember he'd refused to tell me his family name. I watched his face go from casual to puzzled to amused in that much time. "You figured it out," he said. "I'd congratulate you if it was a big accomplishment."

"Well, now that I know, I want you to tell me why you thought I should have known before."

He nodded in concession. "My mom told me I should show up to help you move in, which I think I told you at the time. I *thought* my mom had told you to expect me, but I also thought she told me you weren't going to have anyone else helping. She may have just led me to believe those things. Lawyers can be tricky. And so can mothers who like to meddle."

"Speaking of your mom," Sarah said. "What does she want this week?" She gestured to her display cooler.

"Blue," Jackson said. "So maybe that one or that one?"

Sarah nodded and turned to pick one.

Jackson paid for it but left it sitting on the table. "So ladies, someone distracted me when I first came in," he paused to narrow his eyes playfully at me, "but I meant to tell you some big news."

"Ella had her baby!?" Sarah guessed.

"No." He appeared apologetic in the face of her excitement. "I think you missed the sarcasm when I said the news was big. Noah talked Dan into bringing back... the pizza burrito."

Sarah laughed knowingly.

"The what?" I asked.

"Noah is always trying to come up with something new – Dan calls it reinventing the wheel – but every now and then he'll go along with something if it sounds like enough of a novelty that it'll bring in curious customers."

Sarah laughed again. "The pizza burrito was the worst. Why would he bring that back?"

"Because it was the worst," Jackson said. "It's kind of infamous. It's been a few years – maybe three? – and people will still occasionally come in and joke about getting one. Dan thinks if

90

he puts it on the menu for a few weeks, it'll bring in everyone who missed it the first time. I was at school so I'll be in that line."

"That does sound like something I'd want to try just to see what everyone's talking about," I said. Jackson had said he didn't try it so I asked Sarah what was wrong with the pizza burrito.

"It actually tasted pretty good," she said. "It was just nearly impossible to eat. Picture a big tortilla filled with more pizza sauce than necessary and some cheese and toppings but not enough cheese to hold it all together. If you picked it up, you had to use two hands to keep it from flopping over and splitting open and the sauce still wasn't contained. The top of the tortilla got kind of hard in the oven so it was difficult to bite or cut with a fork. It would tear in unexpected places and… it was sooo messy. I needed several napkins and my brother got sauce all over his shirt."

Jackson was entertained by her description. "Sounds like I'm going to have fun watching people try to eat it."

"I'll skip it this time," Sarah said.

"What about you, Cassidy? Do you want me to let you know when it's on the menu?"

"Yeah. I'm curious now," I said, though I did not like the thought of trying to eat it in front of Jackson.

"Cool." He picked up the flowers to leave. "I'll see you both tomorrow, right?"

We both nodded, and I think Sarah and I were looking forward to it more than the previous Friday.

*J*ojo brought me a flower. The one I drew for him had loopy petals. He drew me a violent storm of straight lines over a longer one for the stem. It was beautiful. He pressed the sticky note onto the corner of my desk, ran his hands over the wall that was still a wall and not a door, and left again just before Simon came in.

Simon needed to tell me that package he'd been expecting had been successfully delivered to his door. I didn't need to worry about it. I guessed I could have told him I hadn't been all that worried. I just thanked him for letting me know. He paused to comment on an interesting knickknack.

I walked out with Sarah when we both closed for the day. We hadn't talked a lot. We'd both been fairly busy. But even when there were no customers, the silence was more comfortable. It was beginning to feel more like two people who weren't super chatty and less like two people purposefully ignoring each other.

Sarah was the first person I saw at the church group that night, too. She was entering the building as I pulled into the parking lot. I was arriving less early than the first week and happy to know at least one single person was ahead of me.

The two women in the hallway greeted me by name as though I was already a regular. The room had a relaxed vibe as I entered. Everyone smiled to see me, and Emily waved. Other than Sarah, she and Gabriel and Ruth were the only people in the room. Those were the names I best remembered, which added to me being happy to see them. I'd barely sat down when Jackson and Noah came in. I guessed I remembered those names pretty well.

"Where is everyone?" Jackson asked the room at large.

He got a few shrugs.

"They're missing out on the news that Ella just went to the hospital." His grin gave away that this was good news before he added, "I'll probably have a nephew sometime tonight."

Emily squealed in delight.

"What!?" Ruth exclaimed. "Why didn't she tell me?" She reached into her bag and pulled out a phone. Her flying fingers suggested Ella was about to get a message with exclamation points.

I was sitting between Emily and Sarah. Jackson took the seat on Sarah's other side with Noah next to him. I noticed that Jackson could have chosen a chair next to anyone else, and I wondered if sitting near Sarah meant anything. Another young woman came in before I had much time to wonder about it. I didn't think I'd met her before.

"Hi, Eve," Emily called to her.

"You just missed the exciting news," Noah said.

The newcomer had a wide pink headband holding back her stick-straight hair. She sighed loudly as she said, "The return of the pizza burrito is not that exciting."

Jackson laughed, and I was glad I wasn't the only one.

"Not that news," Noah said.

"Sounds like Ella's having her baby," Emily said. She looked at Jackson as Eve took a seat. "When did she leave for the hospital?"

"I don't know exactly," he said. "My mom told me Ella went to the hospital because she thought she was in labor. Then I got a text from Ella saying she was at the hospital, but I shouldn't tell Mom yet in case it was a false alarm." He paused to share in the amusement over the contradiction before he added, "Neither of them mentioned a time."

"We'll add a prayer for a safe delivery regardless," Gabriel said. He appeared to be making a note as he spoke.

"By the way, Eve, this is Cassidy." Emily pointed between us to make the introduction.

Eve leaned towards me. "Cassidy *Johnson*?"

"Uh, well, Evelyn Johnson was my grandmother, but she's my mom's mom. My last name is Bodner."

"Right. But you're the one my brother is living over now? I hope someone told you he had to move because of his music. Is it driving you nuts yet?"

"I... haven't really... heard any music." I answered slowly because I didn't know if she meant the banging noises. I didn't know if Simon knew we heard that, which made it feel like something I shouldn't mention. Or at least that I shouldn't be the first person to mention it. I glanced at Sarah to see if she would say anything about the noises we'd heard. She appeared to be biting her fingernail. I could tell from her dancing eyes that she was actually trying to cover a smile she couldn't fully squelch. I looked away before it made me laugh, too.

"I think Simon's songs are really good," Ruth said.

"Oh, yeah." Eve seemed concerned about being misunderstood. "I can admit I have a talented brother. We're all impressed with how many he's sold. It's just that he has to play each song about a zillion times before he's happy with it. Seriously, have any of you ever listened to the same song for three hours straight?"

A few sympathetic expressions popped up.

I shook my head. "I haven't heard anything like that from upstairs."

"Maybe he's finally figured out how headphones work," Eve quipped.

"Or maybe..." Sarah checked to see if anyone else was coming in. "Maybe he's trying to be extra nice to Cassidy."

Her tone implied an ulterior motive that Emily immediately picked up. "You think Simon is interested in Cassidy?"

Everyone else seemed to be looking at me for confirmation. I only shrugged because I was as surprised as they were by the insinuation.

"Well," Sarah said, "he came in to say a package might accidentally get delivered to Cassidy's door and again to say it wasn't *and* he took two trips to return a pan and... it just seems like he might be making up excuses to visit her."

Most of the eyes in the room still expected me to confirm Simon's motivation. I guessed I'd assumed he was somewhat scatterbrained and simply popped in as thoughts occurred to him. This new idea that someone who looked like Simon might have found me attractive was causing a grin I couldn't suppress. It was too flattering. But I just shrugged again because it was still possible that Sarah was wrong. I held Jackson's gaze the longest. It was

95

clear he didn't like my shrug. The fact that he expected me to know what someone else was thinking kind of annoyed me.

"Moving on," Gabriel said. "Looks like we all fit in one room today so I'll get us started."

He led us in a nice prayer I only partially appreciated because only part of my mind was on it. The other part was still wondering if Simon really had been making up excuses to see me. When Gabriel finished, he motioned for Ruth to take over.

"We're going to talk about a saint named St. Anne Line today," she said. "Who wants to guess why?"

"Oh, did she invent some obscure kitchen gadget?" Emily asked.

Her question brought me fully back into the moment with the confusion it caused. I had no idea why so many people thought it was funny or how Ruth could say it was a good guess without sounding at all sarcastic.

"The real reason," Ruth said, "is because Gabriel has been reading comic books."

"Did she invent comic books?" Jackson asked.

"No. She was in a comic book."

"There are comic books about saints?" Noah sounded very interested.

Eve was playfully disapproving. "Aren't you too old to read comic books?"

"There are some really good ones," Gabriel said. "I'll send you a list."

"You're never too old to enjoy something enjoyable," Jackson said.

I was impressed by the observation but wasn't entirely sure I should be. I turned to Sarah. "Was that super profound or just... nonsense?"

She mouthed Jackson's words while she considered.

Jackson answered first. "It isn't profound as much as it's obvious. Something that is enjoyable is by definition something that is enjoyed."

"Except that enjoyment is entirely subjective," Eve said. "People enjoy different things. And something that is enjoyable to a four-year-old is usually not something enjoyable by someone who is..." She pointed at Noah. "Are you twenty-five or twenty-six?"

"Twenty-five," he said. "And I actually don't think there are many four-year-olds who can read comic books."

"I didn't say they read comic books," Eve said. "I said they *enjoy* them."

"Because of the pictures," Emily added.

"So I think you guys are saying," I paused a moment to formulate my thought, "that the definition of enjoyable is not something that is enjoyed but something that *can be* enjoyed."

"Regardless of age," Noah interjected.

"But I'm not sure what that does to the, um, profoundness of what Jackson said earlier," I said.

"Nothing," Jackson said.

"Only because I'm starting to think it wasn't that profound to begin with."

Jackson gave Noah a light punch on the arm for his comment.

"Hey! I'm just trying to figure out if I'm allowed to read the books Gabriel's going to recommend."

"Like you need my permission for anything." Eve scrunched up her face as though she was thinking about sticking out her tongue at the guy she accused of being too old for something.

"Are you two related?" I asked.

"He's my cousin," Eve said.

Noah pretended to look horrified. "Do I want to know what gave it away?"

"Uh... I was actually kidding," I said. "I just thought you were acting like siblings."

"I want to get back to the original question," Emily said.

"You mean why we're discussing St. Anne Line?" Gabriel sounded doubtful.

"Maybe not that far back." Emily waved her hand in a circle to gather her thoughts faster. "I mean the thing about being too old for something fun. I remember being told... when I was in sixth grade, I wanted to do VBS again, and nobody would let me sign up because I was too old, and I must have been... sixth grade? Eleven, I think. Are we, as a culture, in too much of a hurry to make kids grow up if we're telling eleven-year-olds they can't participate in a kids' program?"

"That's an interesting point," Ruth said. "VBS is designed for a range of ages, but kids develop a bit differently. You might've still enjoyed it, but there also might have been a fifth-grader that same year who thought it was babyish."

"Then why did he get to participate, and I didn't?" Emily gave a mock pout before she continued. "I'm kidding, but that's kind of my point about having age cut-offs and... Okay, maybe talking about making kids grow up too fast is too much tangent.

But if we stick to the idea of adults enjoying kids' things, like comic books, why is that wrong? Or is it wrong?"

"I wonder if it hinges on the difference between being child*ish* and child*like*," I said. "The Bible says something about having childlike faith being a good thing, but there's also that verse about putting away childish things as an adult."

Emily nodded vigorously at me. "Yes! We want to avoid being childish, because that's kind of negative. A childish person avoids responsibility and is immature whereas someone who is childlike… that can be about embracing simple pleasures."

"Like comic books," Noah said.

We all laughed at the repeated point.

Emily sobered up quickly and pointed at Eve. "I want to ask you something. I'm sorry for putting you on the spot, and I'm not trying to make you feel bad about it. I think Ruth kind of implied Gabriel was too old for comic books the way she brought it up so it's not just you. Seriously though, what made you tell Noah he was too old, just for the sake of discussion?"

"Hmm." Eve didn't appear upset to be on the spot. She gave real thought to the question before she began to speak slowly. "Well, I think… I think I was trying to give him a hard time about his level of intelligence. I think I was speaking from an assumption that comic books are for people who aren't capable of reading entire pages of text. And now that I say that, I realize it was probably more insulting to people who write comic books than to Noah. I mean, if I'm really honest, I don't remember the last time I looked at a comic book. I'm guessing there's a range of, uh, quality and even reading levels."

"Yeah." Noah nodded at her. He had the same reflective tone. "Like any books, there's quite a variety of authors. Some *are* aimed at little kids… and I don't think I would enjoy those. But there's… I found a section of graphic novels at the library recently, and I picked one up out of curiosity. It was packed with crude humor and profanity. I couldn't finish it, and I would not want to see it in the hands of a child. That's why I was intrigued by the idea that there might be Catholic comic books, books aimed at adults without quote unquote adult content."

"There are." Gabriel slapped the notebook on his lap emphatically. "And now we're actually going to talk about one."

"Right." Ruth nodded at the reminder. "I think this is a good discussion, but we're going to try to get back to our saint of the week."

I had never heard of Anne Line. She lived in England in the 1500s and was eventually hanged for being Catholic, which was considered treason at the time. The comic book apparently portrayed her in prison, physically weak but spiritually strong. We tried to think of situations when physical weakness could be a blessing. We looked at times in the Bible when Jesus used physical healing to open hearts to spiritual healing, and we discussed ways to improve our own spiritual health. A few laughs still found their way into the deep topics. The meeting was so good one of the women in the hallway had to knock on the door to inform us it was past time to go home.

*O*ver the weekend, my mind continually returned to something Jackson had said on Friday. Ruth read from the gospel of Matthew, where Jesus heals the paralytic to demonstrate his ability to forgive sins. We talked about the physical healing being more visibly apparent to onlookers. That's when Jackson said spiritual health can also be seen, though it sometimes takes more effort. I thought of my mom. She went through a dark time for several years after my dad left. I could see in hindsight how she had only gone through the motions of taking us to church until she found peace and re-embraced her faith.

And I thought of myself. I wondered if people could see that being close to God brought me joy. Or did some, like my sister, believe I tried to do what was right to make others look bad. Were there some people who couldn't even see that I tried to do what was right?

I'd gotten another text from my dad. He said he could accept it if I didn't want to see him, but he'd like to know either way. Leaving him hanging as long as I had probably appeared punitive. I couldn't deny some element of that. I was scared to see him and scared to push him away, yet leaving it unsettled was twisting knots in my conscience. Not being able to put the problem out of my head was why it came out of my mouth the next time I saw Simon Donnelly.

Sarah was helping a customer when he came in but still managed to shoot me a significant glance. I tried to ignore her. Heat flashed across my face as my nerves began to race. I'd already felt uncertain about what questions he might have and whether or not I'd be able to answer them. Now there was a new layer of discomfort. I tried to smile at him with confidence anyway.

"Hi, Simon. What brings you in today?"

"I'm glad I caught you when you're not busy." His eyes darted around the store in a show of not landing on any customers.

"Yeah," I said. "Tuesday morning isn't exactly boom time."

"The thing is… I noticed a couple of cabinets in the kitchen upstairs weren't closing quite flush so I used a screwdriver to tighten the hinges. That seems to have worked."

I nodded slowly, not entirely sure why he was telling me. I guessed it could be part of being not a landlord to stay informed about the apartment. But this felt like *overly* informed.

"I thought it sort of counted as making a change, and I should make sure you didn't mind."

"Well, it sounds like an improvement so I can't think of a reason I should mind."

Simon squinted thoughtfully. "If they don't stay tightened, I might end up stripping the wood."

"Are you trying to give me a reason to be upset?" I asked. I tried to tease him to conceal the fact that I didn't understand what he said beyond possibly causing some minor damage to the cabinets.

102

"Yeah, I probably should have said something *before* I messed with the screws."

"I was kidding," I said, because Simon hadn't seemed to pick up on that. I couldn't tell if he appeared relieved or just confused. He kind of seemed to be waiting for me to say something else. I didn't know much about screws or hinges, and there was only one other thing I was thinking about. "While you're here, let me ask you a hypothetical question."

"Okay."

"If your dad abandoned your family when you were a kid, what would you want to say to him if he tried to reconnect when you were an adult?"

Simon was taken aback by my question to the point that he physically took a step backwards. "That doesn't sound hypothetical," he said.

"It is. I don't expect you to tell me what to do or anything, I..." I paused to register that I claimed it was hypothetical and revealed it wasn't in the same breath. "What I mean is... if it was you. I'm just wondering if other people's opinions might help me figure out what's in my head."

"I'm not... uh... I think I'd need more details that I don't want to ask about."

I'd successfully made him as uncomfortable as I was, and that didn't feel like success. "Never mind," I said.

"Okay. I'll come back if the screws get loose again to see what you want me to do before I do anything else." He was halfway to the door before he finished the sentence. We shared a relieved wave as he turned around.

Sarah no longer had a customer, and she smiled encouragingly at me.

I shook my head. I thought if there had been anything to encourage, I had just squelched it.

She resumed collecting some flowers from bouquets she'd taken apart to create what the last guy wanted.

A peaceful quiet had returned when Jojo blew through the front door. I was afraid something was wrong when he came in at a run. But then I saw his smile. He stopped at my desk long enough to place his sticky note on the exact corner, then he jogged back to the front to place a similarly scribbled flower in front of Sarah.

"Thank you, Jojo," she said. "That's pretty."

He bowed to her while she spoke and then to me.

I walked a bit closer so I wouldn't feel as though I was shouting at him. "How are you today?"

He didn't smell as though he needed any reminders. His clothes looked uncomfortable. I could see three shirts with what was clearly the largest bunched up as the bottom layer. Yet there was something joyful in his appearance, a twinkle in his expression that didn't change or react to my question.

"How's the cat?" I asked. "Have you seen it lately?"

He nodded and pawed at the air like a cat trying to catch a string.

"You've been playing with it?"

He nodded and pawed faster.

"You were playing with it this morning?"

He walked away from me towards the wall behind me.

I sighed slightly as I prepared to explain again why there was no longer a door.

104

Jojo had both hands flat against the wall. He slid them in small circles as I approached from behind. He turned back to me with raised eyebrows and an elaborate shrug.

"The door is on the outside now," I said. "Simon Donnelly lives upstairs. Remember?"

His palms returned to the wall with a slap. That sound was immediately followed by a thump from upstairs, and another and another. A trilling high note appeared faintly over the thumps.

"I think that's him now," I observed.

Jojo turned around but not towards me. His eyes were fixed on the ceiling, and they were open nearly as wide as his mouth in a look of utter fascination.

I burst out laughing. I tried to stifle it because I didn't want my uncle to think I was laughing at him. When he didn't even seem to notice, I let myself enjoy the moment. I was not laughing at him, I was laughing because of him, because his expression reached inside me and pulled out so much happiness I had to laugh. It was difficult to connect with this relative who communicated in odd ways, but I recognized the look on his face as exactly how I felt whenever Simon was banging on my ceiling.

I glanced at Sarah, who I heard laughing as well.

"If Simon keeps coming in here to chat with you," she said, "you will eventually have to ask what's going on up there."

"I don't know," I said. I didn't know Simon well enough to have any idea how he'd react to us hearing weird noises from his place. Maybe he already assumed we heard and didn't care. And maybe he had no idea the sound permeated the floor. The thumps picked up speed, then stopped abruptly.

Jojo closed his mouth and strode towards the exit.

105

"Goodbye, Uncle Jojo," I called after him.

He left without looking back. He didn't ask Sarah for one of her flowers either. I thought he might only take one when he wanted to give it to someone else. But I didn't even know if he knew where he was going when he left.

Tuesday afternoons didn't provide a huge rush of business either. I did see a few customers. And Jackson popped in unexpectedly.

I stopped dusting shelves when I heard Sarah say his name in surprise.

"Your mom wants flowers early this week?" she asked.

"No. No, I'll be back Thursday for the usual," he said.

I locked eyes with Jackson the instant I moved past the end of the shelf. I got the impression he'd been stalling to include me in the conversation. But that might have been wishful thinking. I continued towards joining him at Sarah's table.

"I'm on a break." His red T-shirt with the Pans and Plates logo backed that up. "And it occurred to me that you two might not have seen the baby pictures yet."

Sarah's excitement mirrored mine. "Yes, yes. Show us baby pictures," she said.

Jackson got out his phone while we took up positions looking over either shoulder. We'd gotten word that Ella's baby had been born very early Saturday morning. The initial post indicated that she and Sebastion wanted to keep the details and pictures private. That was followed by various comments from people bragging about getting to see the pictures in person.

"Here he is." He slowly flipped through several close-ups of a tiny newborn in a blue knit hat. "Matthew Jones. Eight pounds, three ounces."

The fact that I'd only met Ella once didn't stop me from appreciating a cute baby. His eyes were only open in one of the pictures. "I wish I could hold him," I said.

"I'm told he's slightly bigger than average," Jackson said, "but it doesn't feel like he weighs much at all."

"I bet Ella's keeping him home for a while," Sarah said. "Any idea when she might show him off at the Friday group?"

"Not really." Jackson had come to the end of the pictures and stuffed his phone back in his pocket. "It might be a while though. She said something about wanting to avoid crowds until he's had some shots."

Sarah nodded understandingly but with some disappointment. I felt the same.

"I guess you didn't bring a pizza burrito with you," I said.

"Next time," he said. "Or maybe, uh... I'll need to get the flowers on Thursday, but the big burrito comeback doesn't happen until Friday so I might not... or maybe I can get one made up early since I'm an insider." He wiggled his eyebrows and shifted his tone to imply a vast amount of power with that role.

I laughed.

Jackson checked his watch. "I have five more minutes if either of you has a burning question about the pizza industry."

Now Sarah laughed.

"It doesn't have anything to do with pizza," I said, "but that reminds me that I had a question for Sarah. Do you think your dad could fix something that had been stripped?  Something to do with screws and wood?"

She squinted in puzzlement.

Jackson said.  "Where did that question come from?"

"Simon was here this morning."

"Simon Donnelly?" he checked.

I nodded.

"Ooh," Sarah said.  "What was his latest excuse to see you?"

"It wasn't an excuse," I said.  My answer was kind of a reflex because when I thought about it, it almost sounded like an excuse.  "Or I don't think it was.  But anyway, he said something about some cabinets in the apartment that didn't close properly and that tightening the screws in the hinges might cause a problem even though… I didn't really understand so I'm trying to be proactive about… if that ever is a problem, would I be able to find someone who can fix it?"

Jackson and Sarah were both staring at me, probably trying to decide if I'd said anything that made sense in my rambling.  I focused on the door behind them.  I hoped the lack of eye contact would slow the color rushing to my face.

"My dad could probably fix that," Sarah said.  "He seems to be able to fix anything that comes up around the house at home."

I nodded my gratitude for her information, but I was still having trouble looking at either of them.  Quick glances told me Jackson was brushing his fingertips over a flower with dense petals and Sarah had a strange, knowing smile.  We needed a subject that didn't make anyone think of Simon being interested in me.  And there was still one dominating my headspace.

"Let me ask a different question, hypothetically. If your dad, who abandoned you when you were a kid, if he was trying to get in touch with you now… what would you say to him?"

They were staring at me again.

"Are you asking for a friend?" Sarah asked hopefully.

I guessed my hypothetical questions needed to work on being less transparent. "No," I admitted. "I'm so confused, and I think it would help to know other people's opinions."

"Have you talked to your brother about it?" Jackson asked.

"Not really. He doesn't think there's anything to talk about. And my sister has already seen Dad a few times, but I don't know much about that because she's not talking to *me* right now."

"I'm sorry." Jackson sounded sincere.

"Me, too," Sarah said. "Family should be a support system and not the thing you need support *for*. It makes me sad when people talk about it as a source of conflict."

"Thanks," I said. I did appreciate the sympathy, but it wasn't helping me sort out what to do. "Would either of you talk to him, if it was you?"

Sarah shrugged at me with a helpless expression.

"Would it affect your relationship with your mom?" Jackson winced at his own question. "That's really personal, but I don't know the history, and that's making it hard to have any kind of opinion."

"That's okay. I mean, I brought it up so it makes sense to assume I want to talk about it. I'll try to give you the short version of the history." I gathered my thoughts around what to relate. "When I was eight years old, I came home from school one day, and my dad had moved out while I was gone. I don't remember how I noticed because he worked late a lot. But at some point, either me or one of my siblings asked about something in the house that wasn't there and my mom said that Dad took it with him and that he didn't live there anymore. That was all she ever said about it. 'Your dad doesn't live here anymore.' It was clear she was upset about that so we quickly stopped asking questions. For years, we all basically pretended Dad had stopped existing."

"That's rough," Sarah said.

"There was no warning he might leave?"

I shrugged at the question. "I was eight. I might have missed something. He was working a lot, and I've since wondered if he did that to avoid conflict at home."

They nodded and appeared to be waiting for me to continue.

"Around the time I started high school – my brother was in college but home for the summer – my mom sat the three of us down to apologize for the way she had handled it. She said she was so hurt and angry that she didn't know how to talk about it. She admitted she still didn't know how she should have handled it, but that she knew it should have been different. Anyway, she said she'd try to give honest answers if we had questions, and that if we tried to seek Dad out or ever wanted any kind of relationship with him, she could accept that was independent of her relationship with him. And she knows he's reached out now. I don't think it upsets her."

Sarah and Jackson seemed to be trying to decide who should say something first. Finally, Sarah said, "It's hard to imagine because I'm pretty close to my dad. But I think I'd be too curious not to see him."

Jackson was still hesitant. "You really want my opinion?"

I nodded.

"I'd be angry. I'm a little angry just hearing about it. A man who walks out on his family is despicable." He took a deep breath. "But you don't sound angry."

It sounded as though he admired me for not being angry. I wanted to protest that. The words were difficult to form though. "I am," I said. "I think it's sort of... different anger than... You sound like you want to watch him bleed, whereas I think... I think I'd rather watch him cry. And that's still revenge." I felt a little sick to my stomach when I said it because I knew it was true. It was the reason I had sent no response to his second message.

"You want him to hurt the way he hurt you," Sarah said. "That's natural."

"Yeah. But it's not very Christian. How do I overcome that feeling? How do I stop thinking that I knew lots of other kids whose parents were divorced who still saw both parents and yet my dad just disappeared? Where was he?"

"I think that's your answer," Jackson said.

"What?"

Sarah was giving him a confused look, too.

"You started by asking me and Sarah what we'd want to say to a dad we hadn't seen since we were kids. You clearly want to ask him where he's been. I think that's where you need to start."

"I agree," Sarah said. "I mean, I think it will be really hard, but if he's reaching out now, he probably expects you to ask why he didn't before. Leaving that unasked would probably make it even more awkward. If that's possible."

"His answer might help you know... what's next, if anything," Jackson added.

111

It wasn't quite how I expected. I thought hearing some opinions would help me know what to think. Instead, they helped me understand what I was already thinking. "Thanks," I said. "You guys are pretty smart. Do you have any other advice?"

Sarah only smiled modestly.

"Take it slow," Jackson said. "You don't, uh…" His eyes darted between me and the flower he was fiddling with again. "Someone doesn't automatically deserve a place in your life just because he wants one. Take the time to get to know… him." The way he avoided eye contact gave me the weird feeling he wasn't talking about my dad anymore.

Sarah asked what time his break ended.

"Oh, no! I am so late!" Jackson waved with both hands and then sprinted out the door.

11

*I* had something new to be confused about, something much less significant than whether or not I wanted to see my father. And yet I was not spending less time thinking about it.

I knelt in the prayer corner in my bedroom, gazing at a card I taped to the wall. It had a picture of Mary, Undoer of Knots. Jackson and Sarah had helped me start picking at the knot of emotions around my dad. I knew the only way to untie it was to talk to the person who could answer my questions. I was scared because I also knew I wouldn't like his answers. There were no answers that could erase our history.

I arranged to meet him for lunch on my day off. I didn't know where he worked, but I hoped he didn't have Mondays off. I thought a firm time limit would make me more comfortable. I hoped meeting at Pans and Plates would help, too. I'd been there a couple more times returning plates for Jojo. Dan and Noah gave the place a friendly vibe, friendly enough for a home court advantage.

I had just talked to my mom on the phone. She was encouraging. She'd carefully avoided swaying me on the subject of my dad. Now that I'd agreed to meet with him, however, she admitted she thought it would be good for me. We talked about Ava, too. Mom believed she was softening and might be open to at least civil small talk. All I wanted was to be able to spend cordial time together in the same room by Christmas. If she was softening, and we had five months, there was reason to hope.

Mom agreed that sending her money probably wouldn't help. I'd studied Granny's books enough to know I had more than I needed for the time being. David was wrong about the amount of red ink. But I wanted a family... eventually. Business would need to increase to cover an employee, and Granny's funds meant flexibility for the future. Plus, I did not want to feel as though I bribed my sister into maintaining a relationship with me.

The young adult group at the church was going to start soon. I closed my eyes for one final minute of prayer. The new object of confusion appeared in my imagination. It was Jackson Sweet. I couldn't deny I was crushing on him. He'd stopped in Granny's Shelf yesterday to get his mom's flowers and stayed to chat with me and Sarah. He'd told us not to plan anything for lunch the next day because he'd be bringing pizza burritos. Sarah didn't take much convincing, despite her earlier assertion that she could skip its second round.

When he came back with burritos, Jackson was on a break. He set his phone on the counter with a return-to-work countdown he'd checked every few seconds as he pretended to record our every reaction to the lunch he'd brought. Some dribbled down my chin at the first bite. I would have rather given up and used a fork and plate at that point, but Jackson had brought it wrapped in tin foil with no other option. He said that was so he could relate to Noah how much trouble we had eating it. But he was too entertained for mere fact-finding.

I got a little fluttery as I remembered him laughing at my frequent red-faced napkin grabs. I didn't know if my own feelings were the issue or if I had legitimate reason to be confused. He'd been picking up flowers for his mom before I arrived so it seemed realistic to assume he was more interested in Sarah. There had been a few extra visits to the store though. Was that because of me or because a third person took the pressure off chatting up Sarah? My brain was really churning on the last comment he'd made when we were talking about my dad. He'd said that my dad didn't deserve a place in my life just because he wanted one.

Except that he hadn't said my dad at all. He'd said *a guy*. What was a seemingly careful word choice with some shifty eyes had made me wonder if he'd been talking about himself. The fact that he'd mentioned a guy wanting a place made me wish he was talking about himself. Except that the admonishment to take things slow had sounded something like a warning. Maybe he was talking about my dad. And maybe I was going to be late if I spent any more time trying to convince God that I wasn't praying for more time with Jackson. Or at least that I was only praying for that if that's what he wanted for me.

I touched my fingertips to the base of the cross as I stood up. I drove to St. Jude's though I could have walked if I hadn't waited so long. I told myself I'd try to walk next week.

I arrived as the meeting was starting.

"Hi, Cassidy," Gabriel said. "If you don't mind standing just for the prayer, we'll split in a minute."

115

I nodded and joined two guys standing by the door. The seats were full. I didn't recognize the two guys, but there were several familiar faces. I saw Jackson, who moved as though he might give up his seat for me before Gabriel spoke up. Noah made a similar move so there was nothing beyond basic chivalry to read into it.

After the prayer, the guys left the room and the ladies tightened the circle of chairs. Ruth made sure we all knew each other's names. I met someone named Brianna who had apparently missed the last several weeks. I recognized Emily and Heather from previous meetings. Jessica and Tori I had seen but hadn't learned their names.

"Let's see." Ruth looked around the room, commenting that Heather was counting in days until she became her sister-in-law. "We know Ella is home snuggling a newborn, and Eve works some Fridays. Sarah is usually here. Did she happen to say anything to you today, Cassidy?"

"Yeah. She has a family thing tonight, an out-of-town brother is visiting." I was happy to know *something*. It seemed there were more familial connections in the group than I'd figured out, and one more about to form.

"All right. I guess we'll get started then. I was sure we already used St. Thomas Aquinas as a starting point, but Gabriel insisted we haven't." Ruth's eyes scanned to take a poll of the room on this question.

I just shrugged at her since I could only say he hadn't come up in the last two weeks. A few people seemed similarly uncertain but a few shook their heads.

"Well… first of all… has anyone read *Summa Theologica*?"

"I'm just happy to be able to say I've heard of it," Heather said.

"I've read a few excerpts," Jessica said.

The closest I'd come was that I read an article about a book written by someone who had read it. I thought it summarized a few key points, none of which I could remember off the top of my head. I decided to simply count myself among those who had not read the work.

"It's a good thing that's not the topic of our discussion," Ruth said. "I was just curious. St. Thomas is the patron of students. We wanted to talk about how we are all called to be students of the faith, even when we aren't students in the more traditional sense. What do you do or have you done to continue learning about the faith?"

We looked at each other to see who wanted to speak first. When no one else jumped in, I said, "Can I say the obvious of reading the Bible?"

"Yes," Heather said, "because it's not as obvious as it should be. Even though I was raised Catholic, I was never encouraged to read the Bible. It's only in the last few years that I've realized the importance."

"I think it is…" Jessica paused to collect her thoughts. "My mom says that her parents were actually told not to read the Bible on their own. I don't know if it's a Vatican II thing or a generational thing, but some people have been discouraged from reading it."

Ruth nodded. "My mom says that was to prevent misinterpretations. Parts of the Bible can be confusing and sometimes it seems to contradict itself. It can be... I don't want to say dangerous, but... we do need guidance."

"And we need to remember we have only imperfect translations," Jessica added.

"Along that line..." Brianna raised her hand to break into the conversation. "I'll go back to the first question and add the possibly more obvious answer of paying attention at Mass."

A few people, myself included, smiled and nodded at her before she continued.

"Sometimes the priest gives important context to a reading or talks about the original Greek or Hebrew words. And sometimes I just notice something, like how we say words that have been said for, like, thousands of years and... God is still God."

I got lost in my own head for a few moments relating to the timelessness of the Mass. Sometimes the eternal God struck me with a scent of incense or a general feeling of presence.

When I checked back in at the meeting, Emily had gone off on a tangent about a class she'd taken in college. We spent some time talking about marketing gimmicks and how trying to "sell" the faith wasn't always bad but tended to water it down. I wasn't sure some of the conversation made sense, but it was interesting and entertaining. Emily was mimicking a dancing angel she'd seen when one of the guys – I'd figured out his name was Ben – poked his head in to let us know it was time to say goodnight.

I ended up walking out with Jackson and Noah again and no, it wasn't entirely coincidental. I think I managed to appear to walk out at a natural pace though.

"Did the guys have a good talk?" I asked.

"Isaac was showing us all up again," Noah said. "The guy acts like it's shameful he hasn't read the *entire Summa Theologica*, then quotes Augustine and Thomas More in the same meeting."

"I plan to be just as scholarly when I'm that *old*." Jackson stressed the last word as Isaac walked past holding a toddler.

I didn't know most of the ages in the group, but I'd figured out that Isaac was the oldest and regularly given a hard time about that.

"You mean mature," Isaac said.

Jessica, his wife, was next to him. "Don't goad them, honey. Mature sounds just as bad."

"Does it?"

She nodded while Noah held the door for everyone. Jessica and Isaac immediately took their two little ones towards their car. Noah continued to man the door as a few others were headed down the hall. Jackson brought up the pizza burrito so I was encouraged to wait for the two of them. He joked that I almost had to change my shirt to be able to come that night.

I was torn between being included in the teasing and wishing Jackson hadn't witnessed me making a mess of that lunch.

"I don't understand why people complain they're messy," Noah said. "The tin foil holds it all together *and* keeps it warm. It's brilliant."

"It's also messy," I said.

"Your shirt looks fine," he said.

"Barely." Jackson was clearly enjoying a memory of a close call.

I kind of wanted to shove him for picturing me with tomato sauce all over my face. But touching his arm would feel like flirting.

119

I didn't know how he'd respond. I kept my hands to myself and put one on my hip. "Stop laughing at me."

"The extra business isn't funny," Noah said. "And she did say *also* messy. She conceded brilliant."

Jackson narrowed his eyes as though I'd betrayed him.

The burrito tasted fantastic, but I hadn't actually meant to call it brilliant so I said nothing else.

"Later, guys." Noah dropped the door and waved as he headed towards his car.

I'd been hoping for a chance to talk to Jackson alone. I dove in before he also said goodnight. "Are you working on Monday?"

"Yeah."

"Like around lunchtime?"

"I'm opening," he said. There was some hesitation as though he was afraid I wouldn't like that answer.

"Good," I said quickly. "I'm... I'm meeting my dad for lunch at Pans and Plates, and I... um..."

"Have you been talking to him already?"

"No, I... decided meeting in person was better."

He looked impressed. "Jumping right to face to face is brave."

"Is it?" I said, suddenly feeling anything but brave. "I just thought... I just thought I might read his sincerity better in person."

"That's good thinking." He seemed determined to be encouraging.

I was determined not to accept it. "It was only part of my thinking," I said. "A bigger part just wanted to put it off. When I said I thought I was willing to talk, he asked if he could call right then. I was like no, we need to do this in person so I can pick a time and place in the future."

"Monday's not that far, and I'll be there. Did you want to come up with a secret signal where you... um..." He began to sound uncertain as he thought about what he was saying. "Is there actually a situation where things get uncomfortable with your dad and me randomly sitting at the table with you doesn't make it worse?"

"Maybe? I don't really know what to expect."

"That is the most skeptical maybe I've ever heard," Jackson said. "I'm taking it as a firm no, with a hint of trying not to insult my intelligence. Is it better to plan a way to end the lunch early? Do you think I could come out and say the kitchen is on fire without inciting a panic? Somehow convince your dad and anyone who might overhear that only his seat is in the path of the smoke?"

It wasn't that funny, but the fact that he could suggest it as though he was completely earnest cracked me up.

"Is that another no?" His tone was wrapped in disbelief. "I thought you wanted my help, and yet you're rejecting all my great ideas."

"I just hoped to have a familiar face in the area for, you know, moral support." I was still smiling as I tried to get my laugh under control.

Lines appeared on his cheeks as he smiled back, not dimples but creases that were becoming very familiar. My stomach flittered at the sight, a sort of nervous comfort. And I knew nervous comfort made about as much sense as me telling Jackson I wanted him to be there without admitting that I *would* like him to sit with me if I got uncomfortable.

I think he knew I was holding something back. The creases softened as he went from grinning to a more relaxed smile. His eyes became questioning. My eyes might have been asking the same question, but neither of us knew what it was. I held the gaze until the flittering became unbearable.

When I dropped my eyes to my hands, Jackson said, "Noah will be there, too."

I couldn't look up. Something in his statement seemed to imply that Noah being there was different. I couldn't tell if he was asking me how it was different or why it was different or if he was trying to tell me I could have included Noah in the conversation. My comfort had dissolved in that extended look into his light brown eyes.

"I won't be establishing a secret signal with him either," I said. I managed to make it sound as though Jackson had turned my casual inquiry into something it wasn't. Or at least I was able to convince myself of that enough to meet his eyes again. "But you can both pray for me that whatever happens ends up... well, mostly that I don't say anything I'll regret."

He nodded. "That's a simple enough request. I look forward to hearing how it turns out. Have a good night." He turned back towards the exit.

I noticed there weren't any cars left that way. "Hey!" I called. "Where did you park?"

"Oh. I live right over there so I walked again." He tipped his head the direction he intended to go.

"Okay. Goodnight." I waved and got in my car with a strengthened resolve to save gas the next Friday.

# 12

$\mathcal{S}$aturday was the busiest day Granny's Shelf had since I took over. There was an event on one of the islands that brought more tourists than usual. Sarah benefited from the extra foot traffic as well. Her mom came in twice to replenish the flowers. My favorite customer of the day was a couple who came in with their baby. They said it was their first family vacation, and they needed a souvenir that would help them explain all the memories to the baby when he got older.

The woman suggested about fifty different trinkets, and her husband shrugged at all of them. Neither showed even a hint of frustration at the other, and that impressed me. But it was their baby who was my favorite. He kept flashing me big toothless grins as though he knew the entire time what item they'd eventually select.

I saw Jackson at church on Sunday morning. He wore a plaid shirt and a red bow tie. There was something so confidently geeky about it that I wanted to sneak a few glances his direction. But I was afraid he'd catch me so I ignored that distraction. Mostly. The recessional hymn was one that Granny had loved. I teared up as it started, but when I pictured her belting out the refrain, a smile kept those tears from falling.

Jackson had been sitting a few pews back with his mom — which reminded me of him ridiculously refusing to tell me who she was — and a man I assumed was his dad. Mrs. Sweet approached as I entered the aisle. She asked if everything was going well at the shop and if I'd thought of any questions for her. It was a quick and pleasant chat. I hope she didn't notice me looking over her shoulder to watch Jackson and his dad join a small group of people I didn't know. She walked towards them as she left me, and I went the opposite direction.

My afternoon was quiet and peaceful. I didn't start fretting over the meeting with my dad until I tried to sleep that night. A disgusting variety of fears began to worm through my mind. What if he hadn't been in touch for so many years because he'd spent most of them in prison? What if he got remarried and wanted to introduce me to his new family? What if he got remarried and didn't want his new family to know I existed? What if he left because of something terrible that my mom had done? What if I lost my nerve and didn't show up?

I must have drifted off at some point because I had a dream that my dad walked into Granny's Shelf, and he looked like Jackson. It didn't even seem weird while I was asleep, but when I woke up, I had to spend several minutes convincing myself that a creepy dream didn't make me a creepy person. My subconscious was out of my control.

The morning arrived too fast and passed too quickly. I arrived at Pans and Plates just as Dan unlocked the front door. I wanted to know the number of plates because I thought I had enough time to tidy up Jojo's place before I met my dad at noon.

"Three plates this week," he said, instead of hello. "You know, if you give me your number, I can text you every Monday so you don't have to come twice each week."

My brain kind of wanted to explode in response to that simple suggestion. At first, I'd been trying to do everything the way Granny did it. The next week, I'd wondered if it might be easier to get someone to text me the number of plates. But then I worried that Granny had already asked that, and it was not easier for Dan. He wasn't always there on Mondays. Jackson was there now. Dan was holding the door open while he talked to me, and I saw Jackson wave at me from the kitchen. I liked the idea of *him* sending me the number of plates each week, and I was embarrassed that Dan might know I wanted an excuse to talk to Jackson more often. I was also starting to panic about having to return to see my dad whether or not there were any plates in my hand so it wasn't a good time to make me think about questions less complicated than my head was making everything.

"Uh... maybe we'll try that next week," I said. "I'll be back with three plates." I was already moving back towards my car. I thought Dan might have wanted to say something else before he nodded, but I pretended not to notice. I was too flustered by swirling thoughts. I was halfway to my uncle's place when I realized Dan had probably been about to suggest I give him the number I wanted him to text.

It was the first Monday I was glad Jojo wasn't home while I did my chores. I didn't want him to see me tearing into the mail and stuffing clothes in the wash in a hurry. He might have misinterpreted my haste as some form of resentment. While I'd been uncomfortable letting myself in that first week, it hadn't taken me long to feel satisfaction in the services I provided. Jojo's return flowers suggested he appreciated my efforts, too.

The rough strokes of his petals had an inherent beauty I'd never match. I no longer thought about improving my drawing and simply drew a basic circle with petals, a stem and two leaves. I caught a glimpse of a familiar gray cat as I was locking up. It didn't try to get in or even approach me.

I was about to open the pizza place door when I wondered what would happen if I didn't recognize my dad. I only had 15-year-old pictures. He might have grown a beard or gained a lot of weight or otherwise changed in appearance. I reasoned that I was early. If I sat facing the door, it would be difficult to miss a man who appeared to be looking around for me. I sucked in a quick breath with the courage to stop stalling.

Noah and Jackson seemed to be having an intense discussion in the kitchen. Jackson had a serious expression, and Noah spoke with small but forceful gestures. I tried to focus solidly on them as I walked towards the back. But I noticed a man stand up somewhere to my right. I noticed that he looked exactly like his old pictures. I needed to ignore him until I finished my errand.

Dan was also in the kitchen, farther from the counter. He was talking to a young man I didn't know who was nodding a lot. All four employees glanced my way at the same moment. Jackson was the one who rushed over to take the plates from me.

"Thanks," he said, then lowered his voice. "Is he the guy standing and staring at you?"

"Yes." I suspected my frantic eyes said more than one word.

126

"It'll be great," Jackson said. "And all you have to do is wave to get me to set off the fire alarm."

I smiled both at his joke and the fact that it really meant he had my back. I was too stiff to thank him out loud.

I turned away and forced my feet to the booth where my dad was standing. His arms twitched as though he thought about hugging me before he checked the impulse. There was something weirdly familiar about the complete stranger in front of me. I got the ridiculous idea that sliding into the opposite side of the booth would relieve the awkwardness. It did not. Rather than tilt my head to look up at him, I stared at the back of the seat across from me until he slowly reclaimed it.

"You, um... you eat here a lot?" He tipped his head towards the counter where he'd seen me returning plates.

"Uncle Jojo does," I said.

He responded with something like half a nod. It was clear he didn't fully understand but felt he wasn't entitled to follow-up questions. I could tell he was more uncomfortable than I was, which I liked. Not that I wanted to watch anyone suffer, but I took it as evidence that he knew he couldn't simply waltz back into my life. That almost made me bold enough to ask what I wanted to ask. Almost.

I said nothing and only nodded at my dad's suggestions when Jackson came to take our order. Jackson stood by the table after he'd written it down, letting his eyes flit back and forth between the two of us. He put one hand on the corner of the table as though he was about to crowd into the booth next to me. Then he walked away without actually doing that. The threat – or whatever it was – surprised a tiny smile out of me.

"You know him?" my dad asked.

"Sort of. I mean, a little." My face flushed, and I reacted to an insinuation he hadn't intended. "He goes to St. Jude's."

"I'm sorry about your Granny Johnson," he said. "She was a nice lady."

"Thank you." He sounded sincere so I was, too. He hadn't come to the funeral, but we both knew David would have been upset to see him there.

"Are you settling in here in Andauk?"

I told him I liked the parish and about the group I'd joined to make some friends.

He said he was still working at the same factory where he'd been a manager for twenty years. Then he asked about my store.

"I think... um... yeah, I like running Granny's Shelf. Except when I'm reminded that she's not there."

"I imagine that's hard. Lots of reminders and memories are..." His eyes dropped to the table at what was obviously a surge of painful memories.

Two plates of pizza appeared in front of us. I thanked Jackson and watched his return to the kitchen. He looked back at me as he put his hand on the wall near something red with a questioning shrug.

I didn't laugh, but it filled me with unexpected confidence. "Why now, Dad?"

"I missed you," he said.

"You didn't miss me fifteen years ago?"

"Of course I did."

"And?" Not my most articulate question, but there was enough emotion behind it to get my point across. I hoped.

My dad looked dumbstruck. "You want to go down that road?"

"I can't... The whole... I can't *not*." My eloquence continued to plummet. I thought I'd be able to use words again if we could only get the conversation started.

He sighed with resignation. "I've missed you every day since the day I left. You and your brother and sister. But I didn't know how... I knew you'd be angry. To convince myself I wasn't being cowardly, I told myself it'd be easier on you if you just stayed with your mom rather than trying to bounce between us. The longer I was away the more I missed you, but the harder it became to try to..."

"What changed?"

"I..." He paused to pull a napkin from the dispenser. He flattened it next to his plate and then bunched it into his hand. "I woke up one morning and realized that my children weren't children anymore. They were adults who I didn't know, and that was harder than anything else."

"Why did you leave?" I asked. "I don't remember you and mom fighting. Was I so young I was oblivious to it?"

He shook his head but didn't say anything.

I looked down at the pizza I hadn't touched. I knew it was delicious yet I had no appetite. "Was there... *is* there someone else?" My throat tightened as I asked the question I didn't want to ask. I didn't want to know if my dad had been unfaithful. But if he hadn't had an incentive to leave, it meant we simply weren't enough, and I didn't want to know that either.

He shook his head again before I could take the question back.

129

As much as I feared the answers, I'd lived with the questions too long to leave them unasked now that the opportunity was before me. "Why then? If you didn't leave us for something better, then you must have left because of something at home. You just said you've kept the same job – a job you don't particularly love – for twenty years. And yet you left your family. I need to know why."

He took a deep breath but simply let it out again when I expected him to start talking. We stared at each other with more awkwardness. I hadn't thought that possible. I left my why in the air anyway.

Finally, he said, "It still matters to you after all this time? I hoped we... I hoped we could just..." He sighed again.

I was somewhat paralyzed by the anticipation.

When he accepted that I wasn't going to retract the question, he gave a brief nod and started the explanation. "Your mom and I weren't fighting. But we weren't talking either. She made me feel like I wasn't good enough. And enough time has passed that I know it wasn't something she did, but my own... She *was* too good for me. Still is. I came to expect that it was only a matter of time before she kicked me out or packed up you kids and left. I was so sure it was going to happen that I thought one good thing I could do was do it for her.

"I picked a day when you kids were all at school and your mom had a meeting in the morning. I planned to have everything packed – and I didn't take more than I needed – before she got home. I expected a tense but quick chat about how we'd keep everything civil while we worked out custody and..." His face took on a pained expression, and it was clear he didn't want to continue.

130

He couldn't stop after mentioning shared custody when we both knew that hadn't happened. I think he realized that, or maybe he sensed that I was not satisfied.

"She didn't want me to leave." The words seemed to come out against his will. Once they did, he kept talking freely. "She saw that I'd packed and started freaking out. She begged me to forgive her for not suggesting counseling sooner and insisted our problems could be worked out and... I had been so sure I was doing what she wanted that her reaction undid me. I couldn't think or process or... I just left without a word."

I didn't know what to say. He looked so hurt by what had happened. The fact that it was his fault made it worse for him. Yet it *was* his fault, and I wasn't ready to forgive that.

When he saw that he'd made me angry, his tone changed. It became more plaintive than remorseful. His eyes also seemed to be looking at me instead of into the past as they had before. "I wanted to come back almost as soon as I left. I didn't think she'd forgive me for the way I ignored her confusing pleas. And I assumed she told you kids some version of what happened that would make you hate me, too. It was all so hard to face."

"It was harder than not seeing your kids?" I asked.

"No. Every day I wished I could go back, and every day... You wanted to know why, and the reason is that I was a coward, a huge coward. Can we leave it at that?"

I saw his anger rising, but I saw the pain behind it. It was anger at himself. I was shocked to realize I felt sorry for him, for everything he'd missed. I wanted this to be the only time we had to talk about the past so I kept going. But I softened my approach as the conversation continued, which caused him to open up even more. I still didn't understand how he could have been so sure that Mom wanted him to leave. I knew on a general level what a lack of communication could do to a relationship though.

I found out that he'd stayed in touch with Granny, sending Mom money through her. And that he'd reached out to Mom directly before Ava. He wanted her permission and to make sure trying to reconnect with us wouldn't cause friction between us and Mom. She'd given permission wholeheartedly and also correctly predicted that Ava would be the most receptive and David the least. She knew I'd be the unpredictable one. I smiled to think that she knew me so well that she knew even I wouldn't know how I'd react.

My dad relaxed enough to eat his pizza before he had to go back to work. He went up to the counter to pay for it after he confirmed that we'd be able to talk again at some point.

I watched him leave and then looked down at my plate and the pizza I still hadn't touched. I couldn't decide whether or not my appetite had returned. I was too absorbed in that dilemma to notice Jackson until he was already standing at my elbow.

"I can warm that up," he offered, "if you want to try to eat it now."

I burst into tears. I didn't expect that any more than Jackson did. I only got a glimpse of his face before I covered mine with both hands. I felt the booth shift as he sat next to me. He might have been trying to shield me from other customers because he sensed I was embarrassed to be crying in public. And maybe he didn't want those customers to think the pizza was that bad.

I felt his hand on my shoulder. I think it was intended as a comforting gesture, but it felt more like he was picking a piece of lint out of my hair. It still worked because it tilted the playing field

132

towards me to think I'd thrown him off balance for a change. I grabbed a napkin to wipe my cheeks and nose.

"Are you okay or... going to be okay?"

I nodded as I cleaned up. The tears had been quick and apparently effective. I was already smiling. "Yeah, I guess... I guess I was holding in more emotions than I thought. Bit of a dam break there."

Jackson nodded at me understandingly. It appeared he wanted to be understanding but did not actually understand. "So it wasn't completely awful or... uh... do you want the pizza?"

I almost laughed. Something about the way he switched topics mid-sentence was amusing, but mostly his show of support provided additional release from the confrontation with my dad. I did not laugh though. Jackson was super serious as he asked about my lunch, and I wanted to be sure he knew I appreciated the concern.

"Can you get me a box for it?" I asked. "I think I want to take it home to eat later."

He jumped up and seemed delighted to do that small task for me. My heart swelled to see it. I needed to find out if I had any hope of catching his attention beyond sympathy, and beyond friendship. My hopes had already gone past the point of disappointment. I couldn't stop it, but I could try to keep it from getting worse.

13

$\mathscr{S}$imon and Jojo walked through the front door of Granny's Shelf linked at the elbow. Or rather, they tried to. Jojo yanked the door open and nearly threw it in Simon's face. Simon managed to retrieve his arm in time to catch the door with both hands. Jojo grabbed his elbow and pulled him through sideways. Then he threaded his forearm and bent it to reform the link. He faced me with a broad grin at the accomplishment of getting inside.

I was glad I didn't have any customers to keep me from missing the grand entrance or walking up immediately to ask about it. "Good afternoon. What brings the two of you in today? Or should I ask what brings you in together?"

Jojo turned to Simon expectantly.

Simon smiled and appeared as confident as ever as he began to explain. "Well, I found Jojo outside my door. He's enamored with that new addition to the building, and I assume he brought me in here to see where the door used to be."

My uncle nodded as he rushed towards that spot still dragging Simon by the arm.

Simon didn't put up a fight. His arm flopped on top of Jojo's as the older man slid his hands up the wall. He got a stern look from Jojo when he tried to extricate himself and seemed to realize it meant he was supposed to feel the wall. Simon patted it with one hand and glanced at me. "Uh... sorry we're putting handprints all over your nice white wall."

"I'm just glad you can tell it's white," I said.

Simon scrunched his face at my attempt at a joke.

"Lame joke," I admitted. "I painted it myself, and it didn't match even though it was all white and... I had to paint more." My face got slightly warm as I explained my mistake. I found myself hoping he wouldn't ask for more details because I didn't want to point out where my walls were still technically two different colors.

Fortunately, Simon didn't seem interested in my walls. Jojo was interested enough for both of them. He mimed opening the door that used to be there, then tapped his palms against the surface.

I'd stopped explaining, but now I didn't know what to say about the minor change in the building because there wasn't anything else to say about it. "Have you been to the library this week, Uncle Jojo?"

He stopped touching the wall suddenly. He turned to face me with his hands out flat and a strangely earnest expression.

The library had a full collection of Garfield comic books. Those were the only books he ever checked out and never more than one or two at a time. I'd returned one for him on Monday, and I expected him to nod if he'd replaced it or shake his head if he hadn't. Whatever he was trying to convey seemed more complicated than yes or no.

I might have tried a different question, but Simon was looking at me as though he expected me to understand.

135

Embarrassment pushed me to try to cover my ignorance. "Oh. *Garfield Hogs the Spotlight* again?"

Jojo opened his mouth in mild surprise and moved his hands to his hips.

"I hope you like it," I said.

He began moving towards the door, hands still on hips.

Simon smiled at the abrupt ending.

I couldn't tell if Jojo knew I was putting on a show of communicating with him. I was more concerned that Simon couldn't tell, and that was why I felt a bit sick.

Jojo stopped before he'd taken more than a few steps. He turned back and bowed to me, apparently having realized he forgot to do that as he entered. He also bowed to Sarah, then waved his hand really fast for Simon to follow him out the front door.

I moved behind them to end up by Sarah's table as they left. Part of me wanted her to tell me that since Jojo looked perfectly happy when he left, it didn't matter that I'd ignored him to try to improve Simon's opinion of me. Part of me hoped she hadn't noticed what I did.

She had a big red bouquet that I liked. I tried to make up for one slight by saying out loud the compliment that had been in my head all day. "That red one is beautiful. One of my favorites of all the arrangements I've seen you do."

"Thanks." She glanced at it with pride. "I thought it came out well, but I priced it higher because it's so big. Do you think that's why no one has bought it?"

I shrugged. "I'm glad I get to enjoy it longer."

"It's fresh so hopefully someone will want it Friday or Saturday."

That reminded me that it was Thursday and who picked up flowers around this time on Thursdays.

"I think he's going to ask you out soon," Sarah said. She tipped her head towards the door significantly.

When I didn't see Jackson about to enter, I realized she might be talking about the guy who just left. "Simon?"

She nodded.

"I think you're imagining things," I said. "Jojo pretty much dragged him in here. There's no way that qualifies as him making an excuse to see me."

"What about yesterday when he mentioned changing the smoke detector battery in case you recorded that somewhere."

I cringed at remembering how awkward I'd felt deciding whether or not it was something I should record.

"And he was totally flirting when he apologized for leaving handprints on the wall," she continued.

"Was he?" I reflexively resisted her insistence that he made up excuses to visit because it just didn't seem likely despite the idea being flattering. But I honestly didn't know if that specific comment had felt like flirting.

She nodded confidently.

I wasn't convinced either way. I did feel, however, that her pushiness opened the door for me to turn things around and ask how she'd feel if Jackson was interested in her. "Speaking of pretenses… do you think Jackson only picks up his mom's flowers for her sake?"

"No. Or, I guess it depends what you mean."

"I mean, do you think he comes in to talk to you."

She laughed lightly. "I'd have to say yes and no again."

I frowned at her, and she understood that meant I wasn't satisfied with her cryptic answers.

"Everyone knows his mom is an aggressive matchmaker, especially with him and Ella. You heard how many times she said *finally* when she told you about her first grandchild. And Ella's like twenty-eight or twenty-nine. I'm pretty sure she's not thirty yet. Anyway, she told me she was going to start sending Jackson to pick up her flowers as soon as he got back from school. And she included a little wink-wink that let me know it was because I'm single."

I leaned on the counter to prompt her to continue the story.

"I didn't mind being open to possibilities. Because I am single. But it was obvious right away there were no sparks, probably because he's younger than me. He's very open and friendly, and we laughed once about his mom's scheming so I know he knows there aren't sparks and just keeps coming in to be friendly and help his mom. He probably also doesn't want to tell her… Hey! Remember how he assumed you knew his mom sent him to help you move? I bet he thought you got the same 'let me send my totally available son over to help you' treatment."

I paused to consider why I hadn't. I guessed she didn't think I'd be a good match. That might have hurt my feelings except that I remembered she had sent him to help without talking to me first. Could that have been a strategic move? I had barely begun to ponder that when Jackson appeared at the entrance. My thoughts instead scrambled around the question of whether or not Sarah suspected the reason I asked her about him.

"Hi, Jackson," she said brightly. "We were just talking about you."

I just stood there trying not to look guilty.

He laughed and said, "As long as you're not talking about Noah."

Sarah and I looked at each other in confusion, mostly to demonstrate our confusion to Jackson. He sounded exasperated.

"The success of the pizza burrito has gone to his head." He sighed in disbelief. "It really drove up business and people keep saying ridiculous things like how it was underappreciated the first time and that it's a wonderful idea. Now he's more insistent than ever about coming up with ways to revolutionize pizza and – you'll both back me up on this – pizza does not need a revolution."

He kept his voice stern. When we both cracked up, his smile revealed that laughter had been his goal. "So why were you talking about me?" he asked.

"Just noticing it was about time for you to get your mom's flowers," I said, hoping Sarah didn't add anything.

She only asked what flowers she should prepare.

Jackson rolled his eyes. "Something red, white and blue."

"Why are you rolling your eyes at a patriotic display?" Sarah asked.

"Oh, I'm not." He sounded sincere. "I'm rolling my eyes at her reasoning. She said that she realized she didn't get patriotic flowers for Memorial Day, Flag Day or July 4th... and that somehow means she needs some now that July is ending. I told her that didn't make any sense. It's like if you... miss Halloween and decide to go trick-or-treating in the middle of November. Obviously, that doesn't work and not just because people won't have candy to give out but because... Okay, that is kind of a bad example. I was going to say it's like missing Christmas and putting up a tree in February,

139

but no one forgets Christmas so…" His eyes flicked between us. "You understand, right?"

"Sort of," Sarah said.

I did, but I wanted to give him a hard time for what he knew had been a rambling argument. "I was with you until you tried to explain why it doesn't make sense."

He responded with a playful sneer.

Sarah laughed at both of us and our attention was drawn to the door opening. Simon was back without my great-uncle. He appeared momentarily startled by the three of us standing up front. Jackson greeted him with a fist bump. Then he and Sarah looked to me to direct the conversation. I guessed I was kind of in charge since it was my store.

"Can I help you with something?" I asked Simon.

He shook his head. "I had a question, but it can wait. Have a blessed day." The last comment was directed to us collectively as he exited with a wave.

Sarah had an interpretation ready. "Ooh… a question just for you?" She wiggled her eyebrows.

I thought she might actually be right. The only reply I could muster was the warmth of a blush.

"Is something going on between…" Jackson's voice trailed off as he pointed to me and then the direction Simon had taken.

Sarah nodded significantly.

"Sarah thinks he's interested," I said quickly, "but she might be wrong." I needed to explain this was only a suspicion so he wouldn't think I was already dating someone else. I caught a nod out of the corner of my eye, but I was avoiding looking right at

140

him. I hoped that would help my face return to the normal color faster.

"I'm not wrong," Sarah said, then she turned to pick out flowers for Mrs. Sweet's bouquet.

I watched her hands while I tried to think of a new topic. Jackson was probably watching her, too. It wasn't quiet long enough to be uncomfortable before an older woman entered. She was familiar. I knew she'd introduced herself at St. Jude's, but I couldn't pull a name out of my memory.

"Good afternoon..." The long pause suggested she was having the same problem.

"Cassidy," I supplied.

"Right. The other ladies and I have been calling you Evelyn's granddaughter, which doesn't work in person. I'll have to remind them."

"Can you remind me of your name?" I asked, though I wanted to ask who those other ladies were and why they needed to refer to me.

"Marie," she said. She glanced at Sarah to bring her into the conversation. "You're the one I'm really here to see. I'm having dinner with my sister and brother-in-law, and it's her birthday so I want to bring flowers. But I see you might already have a customer." She eyed Jackson rather suspiciously, almost as though she wasn't going to believe him if he said he was a customer.

"Mom's order can wait," he said to Sarah while motioning with his arm for Marie to step in front of him. He stepped back as he did so and continued moving to give her plenty of space.

I moved with him, and I knew he went farther than necessary because he wanted to ask why I was trying so hard not to laugh out loud.

"What's so funny?" he said, voice low.

I remained turned away and let out a short laugh when I heard Marie describing some flowers. I figured she was no longer paying attention to me or Jackson. I matched his quiet tone when I spoke. "I'm not sure," I said. "Did you see the way she looked at you? It was kind of like... like she thinks you can't be trusted."

Jackson's eyes flicked over my shoulder and back to mine with increased intensity. "So it wasn't my imagination? I thought she looked at me weird."

"Did you do something to her?" I was kidding, and I knew he could tell I was kidding.

He answered defensively to play along. "I barely know her. I think the sister she mentioned is the one who used to work for my dad so my parents know her a little and we say hi to her at church now and then. I can't imagine I've ever done anything to offend her."

"It wasn't like she was offended so much as... suspicious. Like she didn't believe you're really here to get flowers." I started to laugh at the idea, but as the words left my mouth, I realized that *I* worried he was there partly because he was interested in Sarah. Before I convinced myself it was a bad idea, I said, "*Are* you really here to get flowers?"

Jackson bit the side of his lip in a guilty expression he didn't try to hide. "Mostly," he said.

"Sarah told me your mom... uh... that your mom doesn't think you're just here for flowers."

"Yeah. Mom is… well, I think I told you my parents aren't super happy I didn't take an accounting job. But Mom might be even more annoyed that I finished four years of school without getting engaged. She's been trying to help since I got home by pointing out… options as though… kind of like I just need to pick someone. She forgets that someone might… say no."

The vulnerability in his voice said he was talking about a particular someone. I already guessed it was Sarah – that was who his mom picked for him – but like a glutton for punishment, I asked him to confirm that. "So you know that there's little chance of… and yet you still keep coming in not just for flowers?"

He took a deep breath, seemed to be considering exactly how much to reveal. Then he spoke slowly, his tone a little sad but not defeated. "Well… I can't help thinking that little chance isn't the same as no chance. And Mom does want flowers so…"

I tried to nod as though persistence was a positive thing even though it meant his focus wasn't likely to shift to me.

"There is a difference, right?" he asked.

"What difference?"

Jackson studied me for a moment. His eyes seemed to be trying to interpret my confusion as something other than confusion.

I turned away from the scrutiny. If he could read my own hopes, that would only make him feel bad for trying to talk to Sarah.

"I mean… you didn't say little chance just to try to be nice, right? You think… a possibility exists?"

I watched Sarah wave to Marie and begin to clear away some trimmings. I couldn't speak for her so I shrugged as I looked back at Jackson. "I guess as long as no one is married, then…"

He smiled at me. The little creases in his cheeks had a weird way of adding sincerity. It was weird because I knew it was only the way his face was shaped and had no meaning beyond a physical attribute. Yet my imagination insisted on reading extra gratitude. The whole scene was unnerving because I didn't know why he put more stock in my opinion. Didn't Sarah say she'd made it clear the two of them would only be friends? I guessed she didn't tell me exactly what had been said.

"Hey, Jackson?" she called.

"Yeah?" He stepped towards her table with the word.

I followed, feeling oddly relaxed to have the object of our discussion back in the conversation.

"Would it be okay if I put red and white flowers in this blue vase?" Sarah asked. "I know she has her own vases, but I'm not liking these blue flowers in the mix. You can bring it back next week, and I won't charge you for it."

"You're the expert," he said. "I'm sure Mom will like what you like."

"Okay. Feel free to pretend she liked it even if she doesn't." We all enjoyed a brief chuckle as she set the vase on her table and quickly stuffed in some big white flowers with tiny red ones accenting them.

Jackson took the arrangement out the front door. Sarah said she needed more greenery and jogged towards the back door. I stayed in the middle thinking about two of my favorite people in town and couldn't help hoping they'd continue to go in different directions.

14

$\mathcal{I}$ was helping customers when Simon came into the store. He caught my eye with a quick nod before he disappeared behind a shelf. He didn't completely disappear. There was enough glass and gaps that glimpses let me know exactly where he was, though I tried not to pay attention. I understood the nod to mean he was going to stick around until I was no longer holding a snow globe in each hand.

An old couple was still trying to decide which souvenir to buy. The woman wanted to inspect them from all sides. Her hands shook, and I assumed that was the reason she didn't try to hold them herself. But when her husband tried to remove them from the shelf, she stopped him with a stern admonishment about grubby fingerprints before she asked if I would hold them in front of her.

She examined both globes from every possible angle before selecting the one with the monument. I set the other aside to wipe off before I put it back. The woman had me wondering what *my* fingerprints might have done to it. The pair walked out slowly, appreciating Sarah's flowers on the way.

I pulled a dust cloth from a drawer in my desk and began to buff the base of the globe. I was thinking about how to get it to the shelf without undoing my cleaning, and also still tracking Simon out of the corner of my eye so I knew he was approaching. I smiled at him, then dropped my eyes as though I needed to pay close attention to my hands. Given that the item was fragile, the move wasn't entirely due to nerves.

He reached me as the door closed behind my last customers. He pointed to the snow globe. "What happened to that?"

"Nothing. I don't think. I'm just making sure it doesn't have smudges all over it. Do you think it'd be better to carry it with the cloth or wipe it off again after I put it back?"

Simon shrugged as though it didn't matter.

It didn't matter, but now I was a little annoyed that he'd shrugged off my attempt to start a conversation.

"I meant, why is it upside-down?"

I stopped cleaning the glass – that probably wasn't going to get any cleaner – to look at it. "It's not upside-down," I said. It was round on top. How could he think it would stand up if I turned it over?

"The boat on the inside," he said, jabbing a finger at it. "It looked like it had broken off and tipped over at first, but I see now it's supposed to be like that."

I gave it a shake to confirm that everything was still attached. I watched the glitter swirl around the tiny boat pulled up on the sand. "It's not in the water," I observed. "Is that not how people store boats?"

He shrugged again.

I sighed and wrapped the cloth around the globe to carry it to the shelf. I had to touch it to get it unwrapped without dropping it. Then I wiped it off again. It was probably the cleanest item in the shop. I tried to appear confident when I turned to face Simon, who had followed me to the shelf. "Was there a particular reason you stopped in today?"

"Uh... yeah." He reached up to rub the back of his neck.

The action caused his shirt sleeve to slide up and expose a nicely toned bicep. I quickly brought my eyes back to his face, where dark lashes blinked at me and did not stop the growing flush.

"I wanted to ask about your uncle," Simon said. "Jojo. Is he really your uncle?"

"Yes. I mean, technically my great-uncle."

He nodded. "I thought he seemed a lot older than you. Anyway, I, uh... after we left here yesterday, he seemed to want to ask me about the new outside door again."

"Okay," I said into the pause to prompt him to continue.

"Well, I wanted your opinion on... he's asked me about the door before, and I keep telling him the same thing. Is it, I don't know, condescending or something to keep saying the same thing to him when I'm pretty sure he understood me the first time?"

I shrugged. And then I kicked myself for doing what had annoyed me a minute ago. "There are a lot of things I'm not sure about when it comes to Uncle Jojo," I admitted, "but I generally assume that if he asks the same question over and over, he wants the same answer over and over. Or at least some version of it."

"I suppose that makes sense."

"He's pretty easy-going. If you ever accidentally offend him, he'll forgive you in, like, a minute. If it takes that long."

Simon nodded his appreciation. "I'll still try not to but that's good to know. I hadn't interacted with him much beyond waving until I moved in. They all look weird upside-down." He'd been looking at the globe I replaced and the nearby ones just like it.

I guessed he wasn't convinced that was the way to leave an unused rowboat, and I had never had one. I shrugged at him again.

"Well, enjoy the rest of your day. I'm going to see if I can get some work done."

We exchanged farewells before I followed him to the front and stopped near Sarah as he continued outside.

"Did he ask you out?" Sarah didn't even wait until the door was completely closed.

I watched Simon for any sign he had heard before I shook my head.

"Maybe next time," she said.

I didn't know what to say because I realized I wasn't disappointed he hadn't asked. I was relieved.

She tipped her head at me. "Why do you look relieved?"

I made a mental note to never play poker with Sarah. "I'm not sure. Maybe if I got to know him better. He seems really nice. I just… I feel intimidated by him."

"Hmm." Sarah looked at me shrewdly, perhaps too shrewdly, because she said, "Does this have anything to do with you asking me about Jackson yesterday?"

I laughed. Being intimidated by Simon obviously had nothing to do with Jackson, but I knew what she meant. Now that I knew she wasn't interested in Jackson, I didn't mind her knowing that I was. She did not appear to suspect that Jackson liked her though, and that was why I wanted to tread carefully. A love triangle was like a three-lane roundabout. No one entered either willingly, and few people exited without significant damage to the heart.

"Well..." I started slowly. "I guess as long as I'm so thoroughly single, it's a good idea to consider all the options."

"It occurred to me after we talked that he's closer to your age." She smiled knowingly. "He's not drop-dead gorgeous like Simon, but he is cute. And I'm not sure I can think of anyone who likes to help people as much as he does."

I tried not to be overly enthusiastic with my nod. It almost sounded as though she was talking herself into liking him.

"I'm not much of a matchmaker." Sarah stared into space for a moment. "If we could get you more on his mom's radar, maybe with the flowers somehow... I bet she'd have an idea about..."

No scream came out of my mouth, which kind of surprised me. I had to stop Sarah from adding a lane to this roundabout. "Mrs. Sweet doesn't need to be involved. I'm sure she's too busy and... and..."

Sarah chuckled at my stammering. "Relax, Cassidy. I'm not going to tell her anything. I just know she's already trying to pair Jackson with someone, so we should keep an eye open for any opportunity she might create. On her own."

"Oh. Okay."

"Man. You're further gone on Jackson than I thought."

I was definitely not going to play poker with Sarah anytime soon.

****

There was no poker at the Friday night meeting. The toddlers in the hallway were picking up foam blocks and throwing

149

them over the gate for one of the women to toss back. One girl with blonde curls was laughing hysterically. She was so cute. She put a pang in my heart for a kid of my own someday. A feeling like that was scary. I wanted to get married so I could chase the feeling. But I was also afraid I would pick a guy who would leave. I tried to simply enjoy her cute laugh in the moment.

I found a fairly full room when I entered. A few people were already standing. Jackson was one of them. He rushed to my side and began to whisper. "Looks like we're gonna be big enough to split up. If we don't do the usual guys and girls thing and you end up in the same room as Noah, make sure you tell him he's not a genius when he brings up the pizza burrito. Notice I said when. This is not an if situation. He's going to bring it up somehow, and I'm telling everyone because I need someone other than me and Dan to tell him he's not a genius before this gets out of hand."

Jackson had rushed over to tell me the same thing he was apparently telling everyone. I'd already told myself not to read much into his excitement at seeing me. Now I could read even less. On the other hand, he made me feel like a full-fledged member of the group and no longer a newcomer. That was something.

"Prayer time, everyone." Gabriel called attention to it being time to begin. It had taken me a few minutes longer to walk to the church than I'd guessed it would.

I bowed my head with the others while Gabriel asked the Holy Spirit to guide our thoughts and words before he ushered the guys across the hall.

Emily waved me over to sit in the chair her husband had vacated.

Ruth used St. Teresa of Calcutta as the starting point for our conversation. It was nice to discuss someone I'd not only heard of but read about. The nun's advice to do small things with great love sparked a ton of comments about where to see love behind any task and how it could provide motivation for the otherwise mundane.

There were many wonderful examples of how loving someone could provide purpose for much of our daily lives. The talk of purpose eventually spiraled into jokes about the purpose of some very random objects. Emily went off for a good five minutes about how doorstops were actually designed to amuse crawling babies.

I enjoyed the serious insights and the entertainment. The meeting, as usual, seemed to be over quickly. I was just stepping into the hallway when the door across the hall opened.

Isaac looked back into the room. "Oh, I should have let our resident genius show me how to open the door."

"Let him explain to you what a hallway is," a voice I didn't recognize called from inside.

"I get it, guys. I get it." Noah elbowed his way into the hall and made a beeline for the exit.

Jackson was right behind him, laughing lightly with the other guys.

"I don't think your plan worked," I said.

He scrunched his eyes at me in question.

"I thought you wanted everyone to tell him he's *not* a genius."

"This was better," Jackson said as we started slowly down the hall.

Sarah caught my eye with a quick wave before she chased Noah. I kind of appreciated that she left me to talk to Jackson alone, but I also hoped he hadn't noticed she'd done it deliberately.

"Noah brought up the pizza burrito just as I predicted," he continued, "and a few of the guys sarcastically pointed out how no one had ever thought to wrap stuff in a tortilla before. Someone else commented on the complete novelty of cheese. It all helped Noah realize how often he'd patted himself on the back and how he was in danger of becoming insufferable."

"Did you have a good discussion on St. Teresa, too?"

"Yeah." He nodded with a somewhat faraway expression. "Yeah. I still don't know how she related to bagpipes though."

"Bagpipes?"

"We had a whole debate about whether bagpipes have a naturally sorrowful tone that is appropriate for funerals or if we think of them as sorrowful because of the association with funerals. I don't remember how that got started."

"Was there a general consensus?"

"On the bagpipes?" he asked.

"Yeah."

He laughed as he opened the door for me. "I can only say no one convinced me they don't sound sad."

I smiled at his tone and began to move towards the sidewalk at the front of the church hoping he'd also walked to the meeting.

"Are you not parked over here?" He pointed towards the lot in the other direction.

"I'm walking home," I said.

He fell into step next to me. "Cool. More time to talk about bagpipes."

I had only a few seconds to appreciate the joke before he switched us to a real topic.

"Have you talked to your dad since Monday?" he asked.

"Yes. He called me last night."

Jackson didn't say anything, just waited to see if I wanted to elaborate.

"We only talked a few minutes, but I think that's good. I think... I think we both know we need to take baby steps. I need time to get to know him as a real person and not... not just a vague idea of the dad who abandoned me or the dad I wish I had. Just like you suggested."

"I suggested that?" Jackson sounded surprised. "Are you sure it was me? That sounds... smarter than me."

I thought he was only partly kidding and also partly worried I was giving him more credit than he deserved. I tried to formulate an answer that matched the complicated light and serious question. "It's possible you only suggested something like that, and I elevated it with thoughtful nuances."

"Right. It's the nuances I didn't recognize."

"I talked to my mom before that, and she helped me, too. She sensed my anger and uncertainty without me even having to spell it out. She brought up that part in the Bible where Jesus talks about forgiving not seven times but seventy-seven times. She said she heard a priest speak on that assuring us that it doesn't mean letting yourself get hurt or offended that many times, but that we are not capable of forgiving as perfectly as God, especially when it's something really big. We need to keep trying. We might even think we've forgiven someone and then get reminded of the hurt and realize we haven't let go as well as we thought and... Sometimes

153

forgiveness can be a process that feels like doing it seventy-seven times. I've been thinking about that a lot, and it's helped me because... because now I feel like I have permission to be angry. It's okay as long as I'm not, you know, nurturing it or plotting revenge. I'm allowed to need time to... to heal the relationship."

"That's really... I'm not sure I've given that verse much thought. It never occurred to me someone might think it meant letting someone hurt you over and over and over. That wouldn't be healthy. That's a great insight." He gestured for me to continue if he'd interrupted.

"It might even help with my sister," I said, though I was starting to fear I was talking too much. "Not the... um... My mom said Ava has been very curious about whether or not I'll start seeing Dad and... I might be able to talk to her about him as a way to restart some communication. Maybe. I'm still a little afraid of trying too soon and getting shut down longer." My self-consciousness was growing. I was sure all this talk of my dysfunctional family was a huge turnoff for Jackson. "You probably don't want to hear about all this messiness, do you?"

"No, I... It's... I hate that you're facing these difficult things, but I'm glad you can tell me about... some difficult things. It takes at least some degree of trust."

It did. I was surprised that thought didn't scare me because I didn't think I trusted people easily. My mind kept replaying the way Jackson had said he was angry just hearing how my dad had left his family. That might be a reason I could trust him not to leave. But I might only want to trust him not to leave. I was aware that people could be more critical – and even more aware – of the same sins in others. I thought I might trust Jackson more than I trusted my own

154

interpretation of whether or not I should trust him. I guessed my thoughts didn't make a lot of sense.

I felt his elbow nudge mine. "Any other terrible things you need to talk about?" he asked.

I'd been lost in my own head for a full block, and he was trying to get my attention. I shook off the confusing thoughts for the moment. "There is actually."

He eyed me warily. "More hard stuff?"

"This is a different kind of hard," I clarified. I could see him relax in response to my lighter mood. "I'm going to an estate sale on Monday."

"What does that mean?" he asked.

"It means I'm going to an estate sale."

"I don't know what that is. And why... is it something you don't want to do?"

"Not exactly." I had already skipped the first one Granny's contact told me about, but I decided to skip that part of the story. "It's kind of like a big yard sale. It's where Granny got most of the more unique items in her shop. She really had a way of finding used items that new owners would consider treasures. I've sold enough that I need to start learning how to do that. But I'm scared because it'll be my first time."

For some reason, Jackson stopped walking as I made that admission. I also stopped, and turned to face him.

"Some firsts can be... thrilling," he said.

My imagination took my brain on a brief fantasy ride. I almost thought his eyes dropped to my mouth for a second when they'd dropped to look at nothing in particular while he searched for a positive word to tack on. The evening was warm but not hot.

It suddenly felt less not hot, and I couldn't remember what we'd been talking about.

"Hey! I'm off on Monday."

Monday. That was the sale that was making me nervous.

"I could go with you for… uh… whatever kind of support you need. Help staying on budget? I have an accounting degree so I can add. Help carrying things? I have two hands. What kind of help do you need?"

"I need to be able to identify pieces I'll be able to sell for more than I pay." I basically said I needed to predict the future, which was a good reason to be nervous. I enjoyed watching Jackson's expression as he tried to project the same confidence in the face of such a tall order.

After a pause and a few blinks, he said, "Yes. I can help with that. I have excellent taste so I can point out ugly things you shouldn't buy."

I smiled at the thought of him pointing out ugly things. But I also thought a sounding board for my own thoughts could actually be helpful. Plus, the more I bought the less often I'd have to do this, and Jackson did have two hands. "It's in the morning," I said. "I plan to leave around nine."

"Okay. I can walk to your house and ride with you. And I live right here." He pointed to the house beside us as stopping in front of it suddenly made sense. "So you know where to find me if I'm late."

"I'll leave without you if you're late."

"Then I will not be late." He smiled through his feigned intimidation. He glanced at his home again. "Do you want me to walk you the rest of the way?"

156

I did. But I would be perfectly safe walking around the corner in this quiet little town. It was better if he didn't know how much I wanted his company longer. "No." I waved him towards his house as my feet began to move again. "No need to go out of your way. I'll see you on Monday."

"Bye, Cassidy." He only took a few steps up the sidewalk though, then stood there watching me.

Eventually, I called out, "I'm not going to get lost or anything. You don't have to watch."

"If you keep looking back to see if I'm watching, you're going to trip. Then you'll be glad I'm here to pick you up."

I resolutely kept my eyes forward. If I did end up falling on my face because I couldn't resist seeing if he was still there, I would not be the least bit glad he saw it.

15

*I* saw Jackson two more times before Monday. Both were very brief. The first time, he came into Granny's Shelf on a break, wearing his shirt displaying a slice of pizza on a plate and a whole one on a pan. I had a lot of customers and didn't get to talk to him. I pretended he was a real customer long enough to ask if he needed any help. He told me he was there to research what I already had in the store to better help me pick out additions. His fingers made air quotes on the word research, and he sounded as though he was joking around. But he walked past every shelf in his ten minutes. I caught him taking a few pictures, too. It was research.

I saw him next on Sunday. Mrs. Sweet greeted me first. She put a hand on my shoulder and said, "Good morning," as she slipped into the pew behind me. Jackson and his dad filed in after her. They both smiled and greeted me as well.

It wouldn't be fair to say I was distracted during the Mass. I paid attention. My mind only wondered now and then if Jackson noticed that I stood up sooner than most people or that I didn't need the hymnal for the offertory song or that I started singing the third verse second because I actually did need the hymnal for that song. Mostly, I wondered if he was aware of being right behind me even a fraction of the way I was aware of him being right behind me.

There were a few pleasantries at the conclusion. Mrs. Sweet asked again if I'd run into any legal questions about the store or the leases and wanted to know if everything was generally running smoothly. She introduced me to her husband. She also offered Jackson's help if I ran into any bookkeeping issues. This mostly seemed an excuse to point out the degree he wasn't using. The three of them couldn't chat long because they were on their way to have lunch with the new grandbaby. That was how Mrs. Sweet put it. Jackson reminded everyone that Ella and Sebastion would actually be serving lunch.

I pictured Jackson laughing at his mom while I waited for him on Monday. It wasn't a mocking laugh. He enjoyed her implication that a 1-month-old was going to host lunch because he knew she was excited to see the baby. And I enjoyed remembering his smile.

There should have been time to read more of Granny's journal. Once I was ready, I positioned myself near a window to read. I found myself looking out the window more than I was looking at the pages. Most of that time I was trying to decide if I should wait for Jackson to knock or let him know I'd been watching out the window. When I saw him coming, I swapped the journal for a logbook and threw my purse strap over my head. I had almost met him on the sidewalk and still hadn't decided if he could know I was watching.

"Good morning, Cassidy," he said. "You were about to leave without me, weren't you?"

I smiled guiltily. I could tell he was kidding and didn't really think I was leaving so I don't know why I felt guilty. Regardless, I pointed towards my car as I unlocked it.

Jackson beat me to the passenger door, though he didn't know it was a race. The same time I pointed him to the car I realized a sweater and some notebooks and other odds and ends were going to block his seat. I rushed to clear it off, but he opened the door first.

"Hang on," I said as I jumped in front of him. "I need to throw all this in the back seat."

"You must not have passengers very often," he observed.

"No, I…" I dropped an armload on the back seat and stood with one hand on the door while I tried to remember the last person other than me who had been in the car. I couldn't recall a last person or any person. I'd had the car about three years. I guessed I'd let someone else drive, my mom mostly.

"Something wrong?" Jackson asked.

My lack of passengers was probably not that strange. My pausing to contemplate it when we had somewhere to go probably was strange. "Uh, no." I shut the door and dashed around to the driver's seat.

Between staring out the window, staring into space and my messy car, I thought I should be mortified at the impression I was making. But Jackson didn't appear fazed by any of it. He buckled himself in as though looking forward to the forty-minute drive. I calmly launched some small talk. "Did you enjoy lunch with your sister yesterday?"

"Yeah. It turns out Ella's pretty cool."

160

"Why does it sound like you're talking about someone you just met?"

Jackson seemed surprised by my question. "I guess... I guess it kind of feels like that." He continued without me having to ask what he meant. "She's seven years older than me and, you know, a girl. We rarely wanted to do the same things as kids, and then she was away at school before I was. We ignored each other a lot. Now that we're both adults and living nearby, we've been making an effort. I think we're seeing that we have more in common than we used to. But maybe she's just being nice because she knows I'll be a good babysitter."

I smiled at his joke. And I kept smiling even when he asked about my family.

"I met your brother," he said. "And you mentioned a sister. You have only two siblings?"

"Yes."

"Are they older or younger than you? Your brother looked older."

"Yeah. They're both older."

"Okay. So don't answer if this is a sore subject, but when you mentioned your sister, you said she wasn't speaking to you. Has that been going on for a while or do you want to talk about what happened?"

We'd just left the last clustered houses of town behind. There was so much farmland between towns that I could see for miles. The sight of tiny trees off in the distance made me feel small, too. Not small in a sense of being insignificant, but in a sense of being part of something bigger than I could imagine. It made me feel peaceful, like whatever problems I might face were also small in the face of God's plan. It helped me talk about Ava without feeling bitter or hopeless.

"Well, my sister was mad that Granny left the store to me mostly because it came with significant funds to run it."

"Oh." Jackson winced sympathetically. "Money can be tricky with family."

"I think in this case though, it was more of a last straw situation. Ava and I haven't really gotten along since... She left the Church when she left home, and that was about the same time I really started to embrace the faith. She would roll her eyes if I mentioned going to adoration or anything to do with the faith. And I had to bite my tongue at some of the choices she was making. It got hard to talk to her without one of us getting offended.

"David had also... well, neither of them ever made an official renouncement of the faith, they just stopped practicing it. I *think* David still goes to the Christmas and Easter Mass and that's it. Anyway, I know them leaving the Church hurt Mom and Granny. I get the impression both my siblings, but Ava in particular, resent me for not leaving. Like, they think I was trying to make Granny like me more. So when Ava found out she had left me much more money, she kind of took that like I was getting a reward for being the *good* granddaughter. She missed the part about using that money to run Granny's Shelf. I had to quit a job I was very happy to quit, and Ava likes her job. She's a nurse. Granny's decision was practical and...not..."

I stopped talking and sighed, not because I'd given a great explanation but because I'd been talking a lot. I couldn't really look at Jackson while I was driving. A few glances told me he was listening attentively and waiting to see if I had anything to add before he responded.

After at least a minute of silence, Jackson said, "Jesus did warn us that families would be divided because of him. But it's still awful. I imagine it's worse for you because it's immediate family, but I sort of know… I have a cousin on my dad's side. He's close to Ella's age, and I really looked up to him when I was little. At some point, he went full atheist. My mom keeps this giant ornate Bible on the coffee table. Every time he comes over, he points to it and makes the same joke about how he sees we're still reading fiction. My parents always say that we certainly are in a way that says it's not fiction, and we're not going to debate it.

"I'm not sure if that's the right response because I don't know if engaging him would make a difference or if it would only make everyone angry. I know my parents go the let's agree to disagree route because they already tried to talk to him. But that was years ago. Has anything changed?" Jackson gave an exaggerated shrug as a response to his own question.

I was in complete agreement with his uncertainty. I'd read and I'd heard that gentle conversion was best. Bashing someone over the head with the faith was more likely to make that person run for cover than pay any attention to the implement of bashing. But being too gentle could lead to missed opportunities and give the impression that God wasn't connected to everything. And if Jackson's cousin was the one bringing it up, he might be searching more than he realized. Perhaps someday I'd be a better evangelist, but that possibility seemed more distant than the horizon behind the tiniest tree.

"I lost you again, didn't I?" Jackson's amused voice broke into my thoughts.

I wanted to tell him I hadn't gone anywhere even though I knew what he meant. My embarrassment at being caught with my head somewhere else would probably make it sound defensive rather than kidding.

"It wouldn't be so bad if it wasn't intimidating," Jackson said. "I know I can't say anything to match the dreamy smile produced by your own deep thoughts."

There was so much wrong with what he said that I had to scramble hard to get out of another deep pit of thought. Jackson's dreamy smile was attractive and generally awesome. He used the same words to joke about me being distracted and slack-jawed. Those were very different meanings. And it brought to mind another unfortunate contrast. I continued to spend too much time thinking about Jackson, who preferred Sarah, and very little time thinking about Simon, who *might* actually have some interest in me.

Even my attempt to focus on the moment with light conversation was related to the dilemma I wanted to avoid. "Let me ask you a random question," I said. "If you had just cleaned off a shiny glass object and wanted to get it back to its shelf without getting fingerprints all over it, would you wrap it in the cloth to protect it or just put it back and then clean it off again?"

"Why do I feel like your random question is actually a test of some kind?"

If it was a test of perceptiveness, he passed. I tried to appear as though the turn I was making required all my attention and not as though I was avoiding his question about my question.

I heard a quiet chuckle before he answered. "You said it was glass so I wouldn't try to wrap it in cloth because I'd be afraid it'd slip out. If it dropped and broke, it wouldn't matter how many fingerprints I avoided. And I'd probably drop it. I am the guy who broke your lamp, remember?"

"You didn't break it." I knew he was kidding, and I still couldn't stop myself from countering.

He looked a little too satisfied by my response. "So was I right?" he asked.

"About what?"

"About how to move the glass."

"Oh. Um... There's not really a right answer."

"How did you do it?"

"I carried it in the cloth and then realized I couldn't get it back on the shelf without touching it or dropping it. And I ended up doing both."

"You touched it and dropped it?"

"No. I wrapped it and then wiped it off after I touched it getting it unwrapped."

He laughed with mock superiority. "Aha. It was a test to see if I'm smarter than you."

Since it was really a test to see if he'd play along better than Simon had, it felt good to accept Jackson's interpretation. "I'm not sure realizing you're a klutz sooner makes you smarter."

He put a hand on his heart to pretend to be wounded by my comeback. "Now that I know we're talking about a real situation," he said, "I have to ask what this glass object was and how it got dirty sitting on a shelf in your store."

I told him how I'd held it up for a customer and how she'd made me paranoid about my hands being dirtier than I thought. I even admitted I'd gone around the store later polishing objects I might have touched.

Jackson was amused by my description of hunting imaginary smudges. Then he asked if holding the items for someone had made me feel more useful than usual. That was exactly how I'd felt, as though I was performing a service and not just standing around waiting to take her money. He understood because of a similar sense he'd gotten from a few special orders. He told me about a recent request to put sauce on only three-quarters of a pizza and how getting that personal detail right had made the order seem more valuable than most. We both speculated that appreciation for those efforts might have increased our own satisfaction.

By the time we arrived at the estate sale, I'd gotten a few more laughs and was even more grateful that Jackson had volunteered to join me. He made the long drive feel short. There was quite a crowd in front of us. Cars were parked in the grass along the street on both sides. I drove past the house and pulled over next to the last car in the line. Someone else parked next to me before I even opened my door.

I took a deep breath, and Jackson nodded encouragingly at me as we met at the back of the car. I tried to assess the event as we approached. There was a large sign indicating the cashier and another one where the auction would start later. Most of the furniture and other larger items had tags listing a pre-auction price and the order the item would appear in the sale if it was still available.

Eventually, I found tables with decorative items that were more appropriate for Granny's Shelf. None of those had auction numbers. Somewhere in the back of my mind, I wondered what would happen to the things that didn't sell. Mostly I wondered if not being included in the auction meant more reasonable prices up front. I knew Granny did a lot of haggling at these events, and that part made me nervous.

Jackson wandered to a nearby table so we could cover more ground. I found a pair of little turtles carved from onyx or a good imitation of it. I held both in one hand and used the other to pick up a miniature grandfather clock. There was a knob on the back to wind it up. Regardless of whether or not it pre-dated batteries, I thought it would be enough of a novelty that someone might want it. I was somewhat frozen with wishing I'd brought a basket and figuring out what to do now that both my hands were full when Jackson called my name.

"What do you think of this?" he said, holding up a flowery cross.

I walked around the table to get a closer look. The cross was white with a purple cloth draped over the center and yellow flowers around the base. It would make a nice Easter decoration. I wanted to feel the material and found a place to set down the clock so I could take the cross. It might have been plastic, but it was heavy enough that it didn't feel cheap. "Yeah. I like this." I glanced at the price and liked it more. "Lots of people come in for gifts, and this would make a good one."

Jackson seemed delighted by my approval. My stomach did that roller coaster thing before it returned to the level reality of me having too many items to carry.

"Do you want me to hold the clock?" Jackson picked it up.

I nodded. But that only solved my problem until I found something else I wanted to examine.

"Morning, folks." An older man with bushy gray hair and a similarly bushy moustache greeted us. The badge on a lanyard around his neck suggested he was working the sale. But it had flipped backwards so I couldn't read a name or title if there was either. "Are you finding some things that interest you?"

"Yes," I said. "Several."

He nodded and tipped the box at his side forward to show me it was empty. "I thought you might like to use this box to gather your purchases."

"Thank you," I said, taking the box. "That will be very helpful."

"Just take everything to that table there when you're ready." He pointed to the cashier sign I'd noticed earlier.

I thanked him again before he headed the same direction he'd pointed. I turned to Jackson. "The fact that he had a box ready probably means I'm not the first person to realize I should have brought something to carry everything, right?"

"Yes," Jackson said. "And I didn't think of it either so it totally wasn't obvious at all." He sounded equally self-deprecating and took the box from me while he spoke as though there was no question that he would be the one to carry it.

Between the humor and the chivalry, I momentarily lost my ability to think clearly. I stared at the jumble of items on the table in front of me without really seeing any of it. I didn't notice Jackson had picked up something until he held it out to me.

"What do you think this is?" he asked.

168

I focused on the item in question. "It's a bookend."

"No, I mean this part." He twisted his hand so the side with the duck was facing me.

"It's part of the bookend," I said. "A lot of people like to have something decorative on it rather than those plain metal things libraries use."

Jackson gave me a weird blank look. It made me concerned that I'd given a dumb answer. Maybe he was considering whether his question had been dumb. I mimed his expressionless state as the silence stretched. I was pretty sure we were both trying to decide who was at fault for the screeching halt to the conversation but didn't want to be the one to point a finger.

Then we cracked up at the same time. I don't know if anything was funny, but it was a nice end to the awkward stalemate regardless. Once Jackson collected himself, he said, "Let me try this again. You see this bird-shaped thing on this bookend? Do you think the person who made it intended it to be a duck or a goose?"

I'd thought it was a duck. Given the effort now involved in asking my opinion, I decided it deserved a thorough inspection before I answered. The brown-speckled coloring said duck, but the neck was too long. "Now I'm not sure," I said. "My first instinct was duck, but it's kind of goose-shaped."

"Yeah. I also thought it was a duck until I thought about it too much. People usually draw the male ducks because they're more colorful. That's what made me think it might be a goose. But then I thought... if a plain goose is okay, why isn't a plain duck okay?"

I nodded at his reasoning. I spent a full minute trying to determine a definite characteristic before I realized how little it mattered. I glanced up at Jackson, also studying the ambiguous bird. "Are we spending too much time on this duck-goose?"

He laughed and said, "Yes. The only important question here is… Is it too ugly for you to sell? Someone thinks it's ugly because they're only asking a dollar." He tipped the bottom towards me to show the price.

That was the cheapest I'd seen. "Put it in the box," I said. "I can afford to bet a dollar on it being exactly what someone wants."

He set it next to my other items as gently as something with no doubts about its ugliness. The next few things I found did not have doubts. I was looking forward to getting some of those new things arranged in my store. We also had a little fun agreeing on a few things I should *not* buy. When it was time to pay for everything, Jackson suggested I offer a lower total rather than haggle over individual items. That worked well. The cashier seemed to think it was easier all at once, too. I had thought we'd stay at the sale about an hour. We were there for three. And by the time I got home, I couldn't believe I'd been scared to go.

16

The apparently not hideous bookend was the first of my additions to Granny's Shelf to find a buyer. I couldn't wait to tell Jackson. I decided, however, that I would wait. I really liked him. To prove that, I was going to stop intruding when he came in to talk to Sarah. I could wait one more day and tell him about the sale at the meeting at church. When he walked through the door, I smiled and waved and then looked back down at the logbook I had pulled out because it was nearly his typical time.

Sarah laughed at something he said. I tried to suppress my curiosity. She said, "There's nothing wrong with white." The words floated back to me because she turned around to start collecting flowers as she spoke.

Jackson wasn't facing me so I could only make out the word vase in his response. I put my eyes back on my numbers when I thought he might be about to turn my way.

I could focus only enough to determine I was looking at a page from the previous year. I knew I had turned back to that page for a reason. Sarah said something that included my name. She had accused me of opening the notebook to appear casual when

Jackson arrived. Her matchmaking might ruin my attempt to stay out of the way. A guilty part of me was hoping for that.

The door opened, and I was eager for a customer to distract me from my distraction. It was Simon. He made eye contact and walked purposefully towards me with only a quick nod to Sarah and Jackson. My hand went to the back of my head to smooth my hair. He waited until he was close before he greeted me and kept his voice low. Both gave the impression he intended to have a private conversation.

I slid my hand over the back of my head again before I tried to exude confidence I didn't feel. "Hi, Simon. What brings you in today?" Maybe something was leaking.

"Well, I... this is sort of awkward." He tapped his fingers on my desk as he stalled.

Leaking pipes were pretty straightforward. I smiled encouragingly nonetheless. I'd learned from facing my dad that putting off conversations only heightened the anxiety around them.

"You met my sister, Eve, right?"

"Yeah." I remembered her from at least one Friday night, though Simon hadn't been to any of those meetings.

"She told me that... uh... some people have been speculating about... or that I've given the impression that... While I'm not explaining myself to anyone else, I think I need to tell you about my..." He paused, then began more coherently. "When a song isn't working, I need to take a walk. I need to physically step away from it. And your store is so close I keep ending up here. It hasn't been bothering you, has it? I can try to redirect myself."

"No. No, I don't mind that you stop in. Except that sometimes I worry there's a problem upstairs." I forced a laugh to show it wasn't a serious worry, and that I was not at all upset by what he was really saying.

"Good. I'll be sure to reiterate that everything is fine and still working."

I nodded my appreciation.

"Have a good one." He sauntered out, sharing a similar sentiment with Sarah and a fist bump with Jackson.

They both caught me watching Simon leave, and Sarah eagerly motioned for me to come up front. There wasn't a way to refuse the request without raising questions I didn't want to answer. I walked up to join them.

Flowers wrapped in clear plastic sat on the table between them. Sarah turned the bundle towards me and said, "Jackson picked out a fabulous bouquet, didn't he?"

It was very pretty. I saw several different sizes of flowers, all white, contrasted by dark greenery. But her comment was still odd. "Are you trying to give Jackson credit for what you just arranged?" I asked.

Jackson laughed. "I thought she was giving herself a sort of sideways compliment. Your interpretation is more charitable. Though it makes less sense."

"He did suggest I include this one." She pointed at something with long petals. I still had made little effort to learn the names.

"She *is* trying to give me credit." Jackson scrunched up his eyes in adorable confusion as he studied Sarah for a motive.

Obviously, Sarah was even more confused because she was supposed to be trying to make me look good to Jackson and not the other way around. "It's a lovely bouquet," I said.

173

She set it back on the table and gave me an eager smile. "Okay. Now tell me what Simon wanted."

My face flushed at the memory. I bent forward to bury my head in my arms as I worried I had been just as red in front of Simon. "That was so embarrassing," I moaned.

"What happened?" Sarah asked.

When I uncovered my face, Jackson was also looking at me expectantly. They both seemed concerned, and I resolved to be less dramatic. I actually thought I handled it pretty well, without drama. I hoped. "Simon found out that some people," I paused to give Sarah a dirty look, "have been speculating that he's into me."

"Oh." Sarah tried to appear contrite, but her enthusiasm for the rest of the story was clouding it.

"He came in here for the sole purpose of clarifying to me that he is *not* interested."

"Oh," Sarah said again. This time with a deep wince. "That's, um…" She glanced at Jackson.

I was trying very hard to keep my eyes any other direction.

"I hope he was nice about it," Sarah said. "I mean, it's sort of good to nip a misunderstanding like that in the bud, but…"

"Yeah. He was… He did not say it was a ludicrous idea or anything insulting. He just said he wanted to be sure he wasn't giving the wrong impression, and we were both super mature, except for the part where I turned bright red at the idea that he might think I'd heard the same rumor and was getting my hopes up."

Sarah winced again. I still avoided looking at Jackson's reaction.

174

"I'm sorry I might have helped that rumor," she said. "You're not terribly disappointed though, right?"

"No." I shook my head for emphasis. "Now that he's gone, I'm just relieved."

"Wait. Does that mean you would have turned him down?" Jackson's voice finally demanded my attention. His eyes were wrinkled again, but the expression was less playful than the one directed at Sarah.

"Probably?" I said with a small shrug. I didn't want to insult Simon either.

"But… before…" Jackson pointed at Sarah. "When she said she thought he was interested in you, you seemed excited about that."

"Well, yeah," I said. "I mean, any suggestion that a decent guy finds me attractive is going to be flattering."

"Especially a guy who looks like Simon," Sarah interjected.

I gave a quick nod of agreement. "But that doesn't mean I want to try a relationship with anyone who's interested. Maybe if I got to know him better I'd… I don't know. Right now, there's just… no reason to… and he hasn't said anything that…and I'd rather…" I pressed my fingers to my lips to stop myself from babbling.

Jackson's eyes searched me as I spoke. He made me feel as though I owed him excellent reasons for not wanting to date Simon yet also guilty for talking about him at all. Babbling didn't relieve either emotion.

My gaze flit between Jackson and Sarah, trying to figure out if we could drop the uncomfortable topic. They appeared to be doing the same. The silence was broken by the crinkling noise of Jackson picking up his plastic-wrapped bouquet.

"I guess I should get these flowers delivered to my mom," he said. He didn't immediately leave though. He reached into the bouquet and pulled out a single white flower. He handed it to me. "Here's hoping your day gets better."

"Thanks," I said. I was too stunned to say anything else. I twirled the flower between my fingers as I watched the door close behind him.

"Now I'm *really* sorry," Sarah said.

It took a moment to turn my attention from the most beautiful flower I'd ever held. "Uh... why are you sorry?"

"First, I was wrong about Simon and then... when he was here, Jackson kept glancing back and I thought I detected some jealousy. But then he gave you a pity flower." She gave a sympathetic sigh. "Apparently, I know absolutely nothing about reading guys."

"Oh." It was a pity flower? I twirled the stem again before I held it up to my nose. It smelled like disappointment.

**** 

My dad called me shortly after I got home that night. He asked if I'd be willing to have dinner at his house with him and Ava on Friday. My first question was whether or not Ava knew he was asking me. She did know, and he sounded surprised that I had asked. I took that to mean Ava had not told him she never wanted to see me again, which was something almost positive.

176

I agreed to the dinner, feeling that it might be a tiny step forward in two relationships. It didn't occur to me until after I hung up that I would have to miss the meeting at St. Jude's. Or at least be very late for it. I guessed it was a reasonable sacrifice. And it would give me and Sarah something to talk about on Saturday.

I didn't have any trouble sleeping, but I woke up already anxious about the dinner at my dad's place. The path had gotten familiar enough in my somewhat new apartment that I could get to my prayer corner with my eyes still partially closed. Getting there with my eyes partially closed was familiar, too. I knelt and asked God to be with me in my anxiety. I woke more fully as I prayed and began to feel better.

Before I stood up, my eyes fell on the flower Jackson had given me. I laid it by my prayer cards in the evening, and it had shriveled overnight. That seemed somehow appropriate. I refused to dwell on that melancholy thought. Instead, I called to mind how much happier I was in Andauk. Not too long ago, I had a job I barely tolerated, friends I only communicated with online, and an apartment with fewer windows. My lamp wasn't broken, but I hadn't used it since I moved in.

It was a complicated happiness, more like joy, because underneath it all I knew my grandmother had to die for all these blessings to occur. I missed her, yet I was grateful beyond words for the life she allowed me to slip into. I stopped at the church to light a candle for her soul on my way to work. I hoped she now understood some of the things that only sort of made sense to me.

Granny's Shelf had a quieter morning than usual, though Sarah sold a lot of flowers. Mrs. Sweet was my first customer after lunch. I think she counted as a customer. She said she came in because she was doing a refresh on her office. She had a plan for rearranging the furniture and wanted at least a few new knickknacks for her shelves. She didn't actually buy anything. She took pictures of several items she liked and told me she'd send Jackson for what she needed when she was finished with her planning.

Sarah and I were both free a bit later, and she asked me about Mrs. Sweet's visit. She was entertained by what I told her. "It sounds as though she's inventing reasons for him to talk to *you* now. I bet she sends him in for multiple things one at a time."

I laughed with her about how Jackson might react to the repeated visits. But inside, I was thinking Mrs. Sweet wouldn't bother with excuses if she knew about the shriveled flower I still hadn't thrown out.

Then Jackson himself burst through the door laughing. There was no way his mom had already sent him. I wanted to let him talk to Sarah alone, but I was closer to the door than she was. Running to the back would have been awkward to explain. Plus, I wanted to know what he thought was so funny.

"Oh, my goodness," he said, catching his breath. "Dan and Noah are going at it again."

Sarah shook her head with a smile. "What does Noah want to do to the pizza now?"

"Wait for it..." Jackson held up his hands like he was displaying a banner. "Wait for it... different shapes."

"What shapes?" I asked.

Sarah nodded in agreement with the question.

"Lots of shapes. I think. He specifically said he wanted to do star-shaped pizzas. And take requests for custom shapes. Then he went on and on about how birthday-cake-shaped pizzas were going to be huge because it's always someone's birthday and pizzas are common at parties. And the whole time, I was thinking aren't most birthday cakes either round or rectangle, which are like basically the shapes pizzas are already made so I didn't understand what that was gonna look like.

"But Dan didn't address any of that. He just said, 'Noah, there are a million reasons we make the pizzas round.' Noah said, 'What are they?' And Dan said, 'Round is easy.' Then Noah said, 'That's one reason.' And Dan said, 'And when we make a million pizzas, it becomes a million reasons.' That's when I lost it."

Jackson chuckled again at the memory. "I had to get out before either of them caught me laughing. It might have looked like I was on Dan's side. You cannot take sides when they get into it. It doesn't matter whose side it is. They're the same. Either one of them will start looking at you every five seconds like he expects you to spout out a million more reasons you're on his side." He sighed at the exhausting task he'd narrowly avoided. "It looked like you guys were laughing at something else when I came in."

Sarah looked at me to fill him in.

"Your mom was here," I said.

"Okay. Why is that funny?"

"It sounded like she was making a chore list for you. Something about redecorating her office and sending you to get some new knickknacks," I motioned to the shelves behind me, "in between moving furniture."

Jackson playfully rolled his eyes. He looked thoughtful for a moment before he said, "I must have let something slip."

"Did you criticize her office?"

"No. Did you ask her if it was a duck or a goose?"

179

He was kidding so he was surprised when I said, "It's a duck."

"Wait. You did ask her?"

I shook my head. "I sold it yesterday to a guy who said it was a duck. Therefore, it's a duck."

"You sold the one I picked out? Awesome." He pumped a fist in the air. "I'm gonna go tell Noah I have better ideas than he does. I need to get back. I'm not actually on an official break or anything. But I'll see you both tonight?"

As his eyes darted between us, I noticed that Sarah had taken a few steps back to fiddle with some extra greenery. She gave a quick nod.

"Probably not me," I said. "I'm having dinner with my dad tonight. And my sister."

"Oh, that's… I don't know what that is. Is it good?"

"I hope so. Except for the part about missing the meeting."

"Cool." Jackson was backing towards the door. "I'll pray it goes well."

My wave was both a farewell and an appreciation of his sentiment.

*I* got a surprise when I found the address my dad had given me. My mom's car was parked across the street. I stared at it as I shut off my engine. That was definitely her car. I didn't see Ava's car. Maybe there was some reason she borrowed Mom's.

I took a deep breath and started walking towards the door. Car trouble was a neutral subject. We could talk about that.

My dad answered a few seconds after I knocked. He stepped back to let me in and gestured to my mom sitting in the room behind him. "Hi, Cassidy," he said. "Your mom just got here."

"Okay." I simply acknowledged the comment. I didn't know if I should ask why she was there or why he didn't tell me she would be there or why no one else seemed to think either was worth mentioning.

Mom stood up as I entered so I went over and gave her a quick hug. "Nice to see you," I said.

She heard the unspoken question in my voice. Maybe all of them. "When your dad realized there's been some tension between you girls, he thought I might be a better buffer than he could be and… well, I'm always happy to have an excuse to see you."

181

I nodded. The three of us sat down stiffly. Though maybe I was stiff enough for all of us. The room was sparse with plain walls and solid-colored furniture, an amazing contrast to my day spent surrounded by ornaments. I noticed a Bible on the table next to me. It did not appear to be a prop. The cover was worn and various papers stuck out the top and sides. A couple of religious nonfiction titles were stacked next to it. My mom sat by me on a couch that was too big for my small frame. Using the backrest would require slumping, but staying super straight added to the tension in my body.

My dad was in a big chair to the side. He opened his mouth to say something but was interrupted by a knock. "That must be Ava," he said as he jumped up to let her in.

I stood up again with my mom. That felt weirdly formal. I guessed that was a better description than uncomfortable.

I heard Ava's voice ask if Mom was there. She must have seen the car, too. I felt a bit better knowing I wasn't the only one missing that information.

"Yeah. She and Cassidy just got here." Dad gestured to us so she could see for herself.

Mom splayed her arms and said, "Surprise," with half-hearted enthusiasm.

Ava stepped into the middle of us with a nod of greeting. Her eyes stayed on me the most. I got the impression she was daring me to expect an apology.

"Hi," I said.

"Hi," she replied.

We all looked at each other, still standing.

Mom raised her eyebrows at Dad in a prompt to say something.

"Well, since we're all here, I suppose we should go ahead and eat." He pointed towards a table set for four.

Ava hung her purse on the back of a chair before she sat down. Mom sat across from her. Dad opened the oven. "I'm told everyone likes Mexican food so I made some chicken enchiladas." He brought a steaming pan to the table and encouraged me with a quick motion to take the chair next to Mom.

I sat down slowly, still largely uncertain about everything, while Dad rushed back and forth tossing a bag of lettuce on the table with a tub of sour cream and a few other fixings. There was no tablecloth. Dad ripped off paper towels as napkins. The metal pan was old and wobbled slightly on its uneven bottom as he slipped in a serving spoon. There was nothing fancy about the setup. It felt homey, yet totally foreign.

Dad finally sat down and folded his hands looking very nervous. Ava made the Sign of the Cross with us but stayed silent during the prayer. Dad encouraged us to help ourselves but no one made a move until Mom said, "Go ahead, Ava."

The metal spoon scraping the metal pan was the only sound until metal forks began scraping plates. I told my dad the food was good because someone needed to say something, because I couldn't think of anything else to say, and because it was true.

Mom told a short story about how someone had come up to her in the grocery store that morning just to tell her how cute her new shoes were. She pushed her chair back from the table to show off those shoes, which we all agreed were nice.

My dad asked if anything interesting had happened at my store during the week. I told him how I'd been to my first estate sale and that it was better than I anticipated. I did not mention who made it better. Ava did not appear to tense up at the subject, which was when I started to relax. She told us about an elderly patient who wanted to introduce Ava to her grandson. Ava had seen his picture and was convinced that an introduction was a good idea.

The entire meal was surprisingly pleasant. Mom talked the most. I had to give my dad credit for knowing her presence would stabilize the tension. I couldn't help wondering how much they'd been talking for him to know that. I'm not sure how long after the food was eaten we were still chatting. Dad cautiously suggested that he'd be willing to host another meal.

"Sure. I'm always happy to have someone else cook for me," Ava said.

"Yeah, but… well, Fridays wouldn't be my first choice," I said. "I've been meeting with some friends."

"Oh. Are you missing something tonight?" My dad sounded overly concerned.

I shrugged. "I don't mind. I just wanted to be honest about it not being a good night on a regular basis." Though I could have been more honest by elaborating that my friends were part of a church group. Ava and I were getting along too well to rock the boat.

"I have to work about every other Friday anyway," she said. "My schedule doesn't let me plan too much regular stuff so we'll have to play it by ear."

I paused a moment before I nodded. My dad wasn't trying to hide how relieved he was that I was entertaining the possibility of seeing him again. I felt a guilty rush of power to have him at my mercy. I decided it might be best to leave while the evening was on a high note. "Yeah. You or Dad can suggest a date that works, and I'll come if I can." I moved to stand. "But for now, I'm going to call it a night. Thanks for the meal."

"She's gotta rush back to the busy nightlife of Andauk." Ava's words had a sarcastic bite followed by a derisive laugh. She had repeatedly called me a loser for not wanting to hang out at bars or dance clubs with her. I heard the veiled insult but kept smiling because I'd chosen the perfect time to leave.

"I'll walk out with you, honey." Mom pushed back from the table, too.

Dad escorted us to the door while Ava began to clear the table.

As soon as we were alone outside, Mom turned to me with a conspiratorial whisper. "Is that nice Jackson guy one of the friends you missed tonight?"

"He is part of the group."

"Have there been any developments there?"

"If you mean romantic developments, no. I think he likes someone else so you shouldn't hold your breath."

"If you need another option, I couldn't help noticing that new tenant of yours is quite attractive." She widened her eyes for emphasis.

I assumed she meant Simon even though I wasn't sure he was a tenant if I wasn't a landlord. "I did not need anyone to point that out," I said.

She laughed.

"But you should not expect any developments there either." I already remembered him telling me that with less embarrassment. If I could get the terminology down, my relationship with Simon might continue to improve even if it wasn't going a romantic direction.

"Well, you're young," Mom said. "You have time to keep looking." She stopped next to my car, which was closer than hers, to see if I had anything else to say.

"I really was surprised to see you here tonight."

"I could tell," she said.

"Are you okay with… I mean, you're just totally friends with Dad now?"

She smiled gently at my incredulous tone. "Anger doesn't change anything, and it doesn't feel good. I know it's in *my* best interest to let it go. But when I counseled you that forgiveness is a process, I knew what I was talking about. Today was a good day. Tomorrow, I might be reminded of something that makes me want to punch him in the face."

I could laugh because I knew my mother would never really punch anyone. It felt good to know she understood my confusing feelings of wanting to get to know my dad and wanting to hurt him at the same time.

We said goodnight, and she moved towards her car. She was standing next to it tapping on her phone as I drove away. She looked up long enough to smile at me.

Most of the way home, I debated about stopping at St. Jude's first. The meeting would be half over by the time I got there. I was sure no one would mind me coming in late. Others had done the same without a big disruption. I might be confused by missed references in the discussion though. In the end, I drove straight home. I felt like being alone. Or rather, alone with God. There was an unsettled feeling I couldn't pin down.

The feeling was worse as I knelt to pray. I reviewed the evening in my head. It had gone better than I expected, yet I was more anxious than before. I prayed until I grew restless. I got up to go for a walk.

It was close to the time the group would end. I walked towards the church hoping to find Jackson on his way home. I no longer felt like being alone. I felt like talking to someone. Specifically, I felt like talking to the person who helped me sort out my feelings before and the same person who made me smile whenever I thought of lamps, ducks or pizza. I passed his house without seeing him. I got all the way to the church without seeing him. There were enough cars in the lot to convince me the meeting wasn't over.

I turned around. It wasn't that I didn't want him to catch me waiting. I wanted the crowd to disperse before he saw me. It would be easier to talk alone if he was already alone. I turned down the last side street before Jackson's house and turned around again about a block later. That seemed better than the probably miniscule chance that Mrs. Sweet might happen to look out the window the same moment I turned around in front of that house.

The walking wasn't helping me relax because it felt too much like pacing. The sight of Jackson coming towards me did help. But only until I realized how long we would see each other before we were close enough to say anything. My legs began to fight my natural gait. Every step felt too long or too short or simply too awkward. I said, "Hi," when I thought he could hear me and somehow managed to fit jitters into one syllable.

Jackson stopped and pretended to check his watch, obviously pretended because he wasn't wearing a watch. He said, "You are *very* late."

The comment surprised a smile out of me. "I guess so," I said, stopping in front of him.

"Well... I can still walk you home if... I mean, unless you're going somewhere else?"

I gave my head a tiny shake and took a step back to indicate the preferred direction. He walked next to me.

"How was dinner?" he asked.

"Fine. Good. I guess. My mom was there."

"Huh. That was... not expected?"

"Yeah. No. I mean, I was surprised to see her."

"So it was the whole family except your brother," he said after a quiet minute. "Is that a problem?"

"I don't think so." I hadn't thought about David being left out, but he would not have come. "When Ava talked about seeing Dad, he was like do what you want. I don't think... I don't think he cares about anyone getting together without him."

Jackson stayed quiet another minute. "And things are better with your sister?"

I shrugged. "We didn't talk about what happened. I think we're back to the status quo."

"Hmm."

I didn't know if his grunt meant he understood that was improvement without being good or if he didn't know what else to say about it. "How was the meeting tonight?" I asked.

188

"Pretty good. We talked about microwaves."

"Uh… is there a patron saint of microwaves?"

"No. Well, maybe there is," he said. "There's one for just about everything, or at least the people who use them."

"True." We were passing Jackson's house, and neither of us acknowledged it.

"We started talking about St. Monica, her persistence in praying for the conversion of her son even when it didn't seem to be making a difference. We talked about some of the ways that prayer can help us, even change us, when we don't think it's changing what we want to change. Some people gave examples of not seeing effects of prayer until they were removed from the situation or like, you know, hindsight. We talked about how God's ways are not our ways and how he exists outside of time – I brought that up – and some other deep, deep concepts."

After some silence, I realized he was waiting for a response. I couldn't tell if he wanted approval of the intelligence level of the discussion or simple assurance I was still listening. I nodded for him to continue.

"And then Joseph tried to make an analogy with putting a cup of coffee in the microwave. He said it starts getting hot right away, but you can't see it until it boils over. One of his brothers was giving him a hard time about how the coffee is not supposed to boil over so he doesn't know how to use a microwave. Other people started poking holes in the analogy by saying you could see the bubbles before they came out the top if the cup is clear, and you can feel the heat if you open the microwave. So it is an imperfect analogy, but come on, you can't really compare anything to God. I

189

can still see his point about just because you don't see the effects right away doesn't mean *nothing* is happening."

Jackson paused for a moment. He continued when I didn't say anything. "Then the whole thing broke down into a debate about which foods can and cannot be properly cooked in a microwave. I think it's kind of fascinating to consider that no matter where our conversation leads, it can always be traced back to God because he's the ultimate source, the creator of everything. So it doesn't matter if our subject is heavy or light, St. Monica or a baked potato. We're still talking about God."

The idea of God being in everything wasn't novel, but I liked the exercise of tracing his presence along the thread of a conversation. It was something I'd give more thought if I was less distracted.

"Are you contemplating these insights," Jackson asked, "or thinking about what you'd like on a baked potato?"

I smiled almost involuntarily. He was good at that. "Sour cream," I said.

"Uh… I think you mean cheese."

"No, I mean sour cream."

"You mean cheese and bacon and broccoli and onions and maybe a *little* sour cream on top. A baked potato can be a vehicle for an entire meal."

I tipped my head to concede that sounded pretty tasty.

"I can't tell you how the discussion went in the room with the ladies. You can ask Sarah about… Oh! And while you're at it… This was funny. As we were leaving, she came up to Noah and demanded to know what a birthday cake pizza looks like. I mean, she said it like it'd been bugging her all day. Noah liked the interest and launched into an explanation about how it would be straight on the sides and rounded on the top and bottom like a 3D side view of the round cake. And he was trying to list toppings that might be able to stick out the top like candles when she interrupted him like pizza is not 3D. She pulled out a piece of paper for him to draw what he was talking about. They were still dueling sketches on the side of the building when I left so you should definitely ask her how that turned out."

We had reached my house. I didn't stop or turn up the sidewalk. Jackson kept walking, too, but he must have noticed because a house is difficult to miss. And because he asked if something was bothering me.

"Not really."

He eyed me skeptically. "You're quieter than normal. You seem... subdued. And not really isn't the same as no. Do you just not want to talk about it?"

I shrugged. "I don't... I'm not sure how to explain."

"Did something happen at dinner or... your dad said something wrong?"

"No, it was totally fine," I said, "which is why I shouldn't be brooding."

"Yet you are." Jackson's voice was gentle, not accusing. "I don't mind being confused if you don't mind telling me."

I had made a pointed effort to talk to Jackson. I guessed it was weird to avoid actually talking to him. "Okay. Well... my mom was there. And my dad hasn't changed much. He looks a lot like he did when I was little, and I... it reminded me of when I was little and... I was flooded with this insane desire to see my parents back together like we could all be one big happy family again, and that's

191

so childish. I don't even live with either of them so it wouldn't really affect me and it… makes me feel so… so stupid."

Jackson was thoughtful for a few moments, clearly taking time to respond. He wasn't laughing at me though. That was all that mattered. I'd been so afraid he'd laugh. Finally, he said, "God intended marriage to be permanent. He intended families to stay together. I don't think there's anything childish or insane about wanting what God wants for everyone. Now if you were starting to think you might get what you want because they had one civil conversation…"

I saw the humor in his suggestion, which meant I could still tell the difference between fantasy and reality. I guessed I wasn't as pathetic as I thought.

"And it would affect you," Jackson continued. "Certainly not as much as if you were four years old. But any time you have a relationship with someone, that person's other relationships affect you. I had a friend at school whose parents split, and he hated visiting either of them because he always felt like he wasn't allowed to mention the other parent when he was with them and that was hard. And this other guy, he started dating this girl who – man, I hope they're not still together – he could not do anything right in her eyes. It was super uncomfortable to be around them. I spent less and less time with him because even when she wasn't around, he'd say stuff like, 'Lyssa'll be mad if she sees me wearing this shirt again.' And what do you say to that?"

"You're right," I said. "I see what you mean about… I think it just hurts that I… I don't know. Sometimes wishful thinking hurts."

192

"I'm sorry," he said, nodding along with my sentiment. "Cassidy… can I give you a hug?"

I wanted a hug bad. But not everyone was a hugger so it was sweet that he asked first. I was already reaching for it when I nodded. The warmth was so nice, way more comforting even than not being laughed at. I sighed out some frustration in his arms. Then I backed away. The mood shifted from soothing to thrilling when Jackson stepped back with a handful of my hair still slipping through his fingers. My breath caught.

"Cassidy?" His voice was deeper than usual. "Can I see you again soon?"

It didn't sound like a casual question, but I wanted to be sure it meant what I thought it meant. "You probably will," I said. "We seem to bump into each other a lot."

He gave me a lopsided smile. "You call it bumping into each other when I deliberately pop into your shop a couple times a week?"

"Well, I thought… I thought you liked Sarah."

"No, I… I mean, I do *like* Sarah. But I like you more."

My insides got so warm and squishy I was sure my feet were hitting the ground lighter than before. His voice had dropped again on those last four words. I let the deep sound repeat in my head.

"Do you mind?" Jackson asked.

I did not mind anything at the moment. My squishy brain still registered that he was trying to nudge a response out of me. It wasn't fair to keep soaking up the vulnerability without offering him encouragement. "I'm happy when we bump into each other."

He was facing forward. I had an excellent view of that crease on his cheek when my answer made him grin. "I have an idea," he

193

said. "But we should turn around first in case it makes you want to run towards your house."

I smiled rather than worry about the idea as I could see the real reason we turned around was that we were about to run out of sidewalk.

"How would you feel about coming to my house for lunch after church on Sunday?"

"Why would that make me want to run away?"

"It's not just my house," he said. "My parents will be there, and Ella and Sebastian will bring Matthew."

"Aw... I hope you're not suggesting an adorable baby will make me run."

"No, my parents. My mom in particular. She can be a little much. I mean, it's kind of why I think it'll be fun, but for you..." He winced apologetically.

I narrowed my eyes at him. "Are you saying you'll enjoy watching your mom interrogate me?"

"Oh, no. She, uh... The novelty of being a grandmother hasn't worn off. She's going to want to spend the entire time fussing over the baby. But she'll also want to spend the entire time trying to convince you that I'm awesome. It might be fun to watch her try to balance those impulses."

"Should I be worried about her saying you're awesome or... I'm actually a little confused about whether you're trying to convince me to come or not."

"You should come," he said, "just be prepared for my mom to exaggerate everything I do."

I agreed to come as long as he stayed close to point out the exaggerations. We worked out the details about timing and whether

194

I should stop at home first. We backtracked to my house before we were done and stopped that time. After he continued on his way home, I went into my house and just smiled. *I like you more.* Those words outstripped all the strain of the evening.

## 18

I heard the wheels of Sarah's flower cart rattling across the street as I unlocked the back door of my shop. In my first few weeks, the same sound caused me stress. I couldn't decide if standing around waiting for her was more or less awkward than going inside knowing I was only a minute ahead of her. Now I wanted to wait.

When she was close enough to hear my shout over the wheels, I said, "You suck at reading guys."

"Oh, I know," she said. "I said I was sorry and…" She stopped when she saw me shaking my head at her apology.

I grinned. "It wasn't a pity flower."

Her eyebrows came together as she tried to figure out what I meant. She gasped as she remembered. "Did something happen with Jackson?"

I nodded and motioned her through the door before we talked more.

Sarah paused just over the threshold and turned back expectantly.

The eagerness made me want to make her wait. I motioned again for her to keep going to the front. Once her cart was parked

196

in the usual spot, she sighed impatiently at me. "Tell me what happened."

"I'm having lunch with him tomorrow."

She smiled. "That's awesome. But how did that happen? I just saw you yesterday, and you weren't at St. Jude's with us."

"I went for a walk after I got back from dinner and bumped into Jackson walking home from St. Jude's."

"You know he usually walks home, don't you?" Her skeptical tone said she knew the meeting wasn't as coincidental as I implied.

"Yes. I was trying to bump into him."

"Good move." She was excited for me. "And this lunch tomorrow is… significant?"

I think she was trying to be sure I had read the situation right. "I'm going to his parents' house, and the way he talked about his mom trying to sell me on his good points has to mean he's going to tell her – or at least let her believe – it's significant."

"Yay! At the end of the day, I'm going to give you some flowers to take with you," Sarah said. "You'll want to make a good impression, too, and we know Mrs. Sweet loves flowers."

I didn't think that was necessary – Mrs. Sweet had already started some matchmaking efforts my direction – but a nice gesture was always appreciated, and I could tell it would make Sarah happy to help.

I unlocked the front door and had my first customer in minutes, and more of them throughout the morning. I was between customers when I overheard Sarah helping an older guy I recognized from church. I did not know his name. Sarah appeared to know him fairly well. She asked after a few people, and he mentioned someone named Brendon who would be visiting soon. I approached Sarah as he left.

"I know I've seen him at church, but we haven't been introduced. What's his name?"

"His first name is Doug," Sarah said, "though I know him as Mr. Wahl. He's Brendon's dad."

"Well, now I have to ask… who's Brendon?"

"A friend of mine."

"Just a friend?" I asked.

"Yes." Her eyes sparkled though.

I waited for the rest of the story.

"We went to high school together, but then he went to South Carolina for college and stayed there after he graduated. We've kept in touch the whole time. I see him whenever he visits his parents." She paused with a faraway look in her eyes. "He complains that it's too hot there. Sometimes I entertain the fantasy that he'll move back home and then… then maybe we don't have to be just friends anymore."

I nodded sympathetically. I knew something about unrealistic fantasies. We didn't have much time to dwell on it. The customers continued to trickle in and out so that there was at least one other person in the shop most of the day. Simon came in. When he saw I was busy, he smiled at me, browsed a shelf or two, then left again. I was able to return the smile more calmly now that the mystery had been removed from his brief appearances. Jojo came in a bit later. He bowed to Sarah, then to me, then to a random woman looking at Lake Erie knickknacks. He was unfazed when instead of returning the bow, she backed away as though it'd been a threatening gesture.

He didn't fully stop for any of the bows and continued towards the usual spot on the wall. I followed him. Rather than rub his palms over the surface, he simply knocked on it before he turned and nodded vigorously.

"Yeah, it's a good wall," I said. "Mr. Franks knows what he's doing."

He nodded again. Then he held one arm out to the side and made a windmill motion with the other. It was not a sign I'd seen before. I winced at how close his hand came to hitting a glass shelf.

Jojo smiled at me. He seemed amused that I didn't understand. He pulled a crumpled sticky note from his pocket, showed me the flower he'd drawn and went to stick it to my desk. He passed the same woman, and she gave him a tentative bow, which made his smile even bigger. She'd only been startled by his odd behavior.

Joseph came in to buy flowers for Emily. He was wearing some sort of martial arts uniform, complete with a black belt, so I guessed he was in between classes at his nearby family rec center. Emily popped in a few minutes later to compliment Sarah on her taste. She was wearing a gray T-shirt and a sparkly purple tutu. They were a cute pair. By the end of the day, I was thinking that Jackson was one of the few people I knew in town who hadn't been in the store. I didn't mind since I knew I'd see him soon.

In fact, he brought his parents up to sit in the same pew as me the next morning. Mrs. Sweet leaned over him as they sat down. "Cassidy, I hear we're going to be seeing more of you later today," she said. "It's wonderful. And Jackson is doing all the cooking for lunch." She pulled in her excitement to kneel quietly.

199

Jackson whispered to me. "It's a frozen lasagna that I put in the oven all by myself."

I smirked at his fake bragging.

After Mass, I went home to change clothes and leave my car. Jackson had told me he preferred to get into more comfortable clothes after church and didn't want me to make him look bad by staying dressed up.

Mrs. Sweet greeted me at the door with a tiny baby nestled in the crook of one arm. "Welcome, Cassidy. Let me introduce you to my amazing grandson, Matthew."

"Aw." I think we both would have been happy to stand there gazing at the baby for quite a while.

Jackson came up and interrupted us. "Are you going to let her come all the way into the house, Mom?"

"Of course." Mrs. Sweet started moving towards the room Jackson had come from. I heard voices in there. "You've already met my equally wonderful son," she said to me. "He's really good with the baby. He holds him... so... gently." The last words came out slowly as her arms twitched. It was clear she was having trouble deciding whether it was more important to her to keep holding the baby or prove that Jackson was equally capable.

"Oh, flowers. Take the flowers from Cassidy," she said, and sounded relieved for the out. I could see why he thought the struggle might be entertaining, though he kept a straight face when she chose to hang on to her grandbaby.

I recognized Ella and Sebastion from meeting them at the young adult group. They told me they'd probably start attending again the next Friday.

Mrs. Sweet said the new parents wouldn't have gotten married if it weren't for that group. I wanted to hear the story, but Ella just said it was where they spent some time getting to know each other.

Lunch was good, the food and the company. Mrs. Sweet mentioned again how Jackson had made it. She also talked about how his degree was going to open a lot of doors when he got tired of making pizzas. She said he was amazing with numbers. He dryly proved he knew the answer to two plus two, and his mom smiled as though he was being modest and not contrary.

I got to hold the baby for exactly one minute when Mrs. Sweet needed both hands for something. When I gave him back, Mr. Sweet commented how surprised he was that she hadn't stressed how much holding the baby must make me want one. Somehow, his surprise conveyed the same thing she didn't say.

Everyone was very nice, but I didn't stay long after we finished eating. Jackson insisted on walking me home. His mom was perhaps overly pleased by that. There was some animated whispering with his dad where I might have heard the word married. I felt a hint of relief when Jackson closed the door on the others.

"What did you think?" he asked as we started down the porch steps.

"You were right about your mom trying to sell your good qualities."

He smiled. "I'll tell her next week she can brag about how I'm good at being right."

I playfully punched his arm.

"I think that's Gabriel," he said.

201

I followed his eyes to find the source of the observation. There was a man jogging on the other side of the street. It was Gabriel. I thought we'd just wave as he passed, but he veered across the street directly towards us. We stopped to meet him.

"Hi, Jackson," he said. "Cassidy, I've been meaning to talk to you and missed you Friday. Julia wants me to ask if she can pay for some cat food."

He continued to jog in place as he spoke and the distracting bouncing might have slowed my comprehension. But I might have given him the same dazed look if he was holding still. I was mildly relieved to see that Jackson was also confused.

"What cat food?" I asked.

"To reimburse Jojo."

"Oh!" Julia must be the person who owned the cat Jojo was feeding. I'd mostly given up on solving that mystery. "Who's Julia?"

"She's my sister-in-law," Gabriel said. "You didn't know it was her cat?"

I shook my head. The relationship to Gabriel still didn't really tell me who she was either. "I wanted to ask the owner if she minded Jojo sort of jointly adopting the cat, but I couldn't figure out how to figure out who that was."

"She definitely doesn't mind sharing Snowball. Eric, my brother, doesn't mind either because he's not much of a cat person."

"Great," I said. "In that case, tell her she doesn't owe him or me anything. Jojo likes the cat, and that's certainly worth the cost of some food."

"Thanks. I'll let her know." He gave us both a quick nod before continuing on his way.

Jackson and I continued the other direction. We rounded the corner in a comfortable silence. As my house came into view, he confirmed – again – that I should consider Sunday lunch a standing invitation. Then we talked about his schedule for the coming week and what might be a good time to get together. We stopped where the sidewalk turned towards my porch, and he hugged me goodbye.

It was a quick squeeze, but when he let go, he didn't fully let go. One hand stayed on my shoulder. His eyes looked intently into mine. I knew what he was thinking, and I successfully communicated in the breathless silence that I was thinking it, too. We leaned in together for the kiss. It was over too fast but would leave a long memory.

We were both smiling big while trying not to smile even bigger as he began to head back home. I got to my porch before he reached the corner, and I stood and watched him. I thought about what he had said recently about how our relationships affected our other relationships. It made me curious how this budding relationship with Jackson might affect those around me. I didn't know the answer yet. I suspected that it would involve me smiling more.

~~The End~~

Find out about upcoming books, read excerpts with notes from the author, watch various covers take shape, and much more at www.amandahammbooks.com.

www.ingramcontent.com/pod-product-compliance
Lightning Source LLC
Chambersburg PA
CBHW030316180626
46810CB00003B/1107